STAR WARS THE CLONE WARS

A Random House SCREEN COMIX™ Book

SEASON 7 • VOLUME 1

Random House • New York

For Lucasfilm
Senior Editor: Robert Simpson
Creative Director: Michael Siglain
Art Director: Troy Alders
Project Manager, Digital & Video Assets: LeAndre Thomas
Lucasfilm Art Department: Phil Szostak
Lucasfilm Story Group: Pablo Hidalgo, Matt Martin, and Emily Shkoukani

ISBN 978-0-7364-4164-3
rhcbooks.com

Printed in the United States of America
10 9 8 7 6 5 4 3 2 1

EPISODE 1
THE BAD BATCH

Embrace others for their differences, for that makes you whole.

THE BATTLE FOR ANAXES! ONE OF THE REPUBLIC'S LARGEST SHIPYARDS IS UNDER ATTACK FROM ADMIRAL TRENCH'S SEPARATIST FORCES.

JEDI GENERALS MACE WINDU AND ANAKIN SKYWALKER LEAD A TWO-PRONGED ASSAULT ON THE GROUND AND IN THE AIR.

BUT AFTER WEEKS OF HEATED BATTLE AND MOUNTING LOSSES, THE REPUBLIC'S GRIP ON ANAXES BEGINS TO SLIP AWAY.

THE DROIDS HAVE OVERRUN OUR MAIN PRODUCTION FACILITY. IT WON'T BE LONG BEFORE THE SEPARATISTS TAKE ANAXES, COMPROMISING OUR ENTIRE RESERVE FLEET.

PARDON THE INTERRUPTION, GENERAL...

BUT REX HERE HAS A GOOD THEORY ON WHY WE KEEP, UH... LOSING.

PLEASE, CAPTAIN.

THE DROID ARMY USES ANALYTICS TO PREDICT OUR STRATEGY. THE FIRST TIME WE USE A TACTIC, IT'S VERY EFFECTIVE. THE NEXT, LESS SO.

IN FACT, THE MORE WE USE A CERTAIN TACTIC, THE LESS EFFECTIVE IT BECOMES.
THEY LEARN OUR TENDENCIES AND USE THAT DATA AGAINST US.
TO COUNTER THEM, WE'RE CONSTANTLY WORKING OUT WAYS TO VARY OUR ATTACK.

BUT THE LOSSES WE ARE EXPERIENCING ON ANAXES ARE NOT COMMONPLACE.

EXACTLY. THE COUNTERATTACKS ARE SO SPECIFIC, IT'S MY STRATEGY THE DROIDS KNOW, MY PLAYBOOK.

MY CONCERN IS THAT REX IS ONE OF OUR BEST. IF THE DROIDS CAN LEARN TO DEFEAT HIM, WE MAY ALL BE VULNERABLE.

WHAT DO YOU PROPOSE?

LET REX AND ME TAKE A SMALL SQUAD BEHIND ENEMY LINES.
THERE'S A SEPARATIST CYBER CENTER WHICH RELAYS ALL BATTLEFIELD INTEL TO THEIR COMMAND SHIP. IF WE'RE GOING TO FIND ANYTHING, IT WILL BE THERE.

IF YOU THINK
IT WILL HELP TURN
THIS FIGHT AROUND,
GET GOING.

THANK YOU,
GENERAL.

REX, IS THERE
ANYTHING ELSE?

NO, GENERAL.

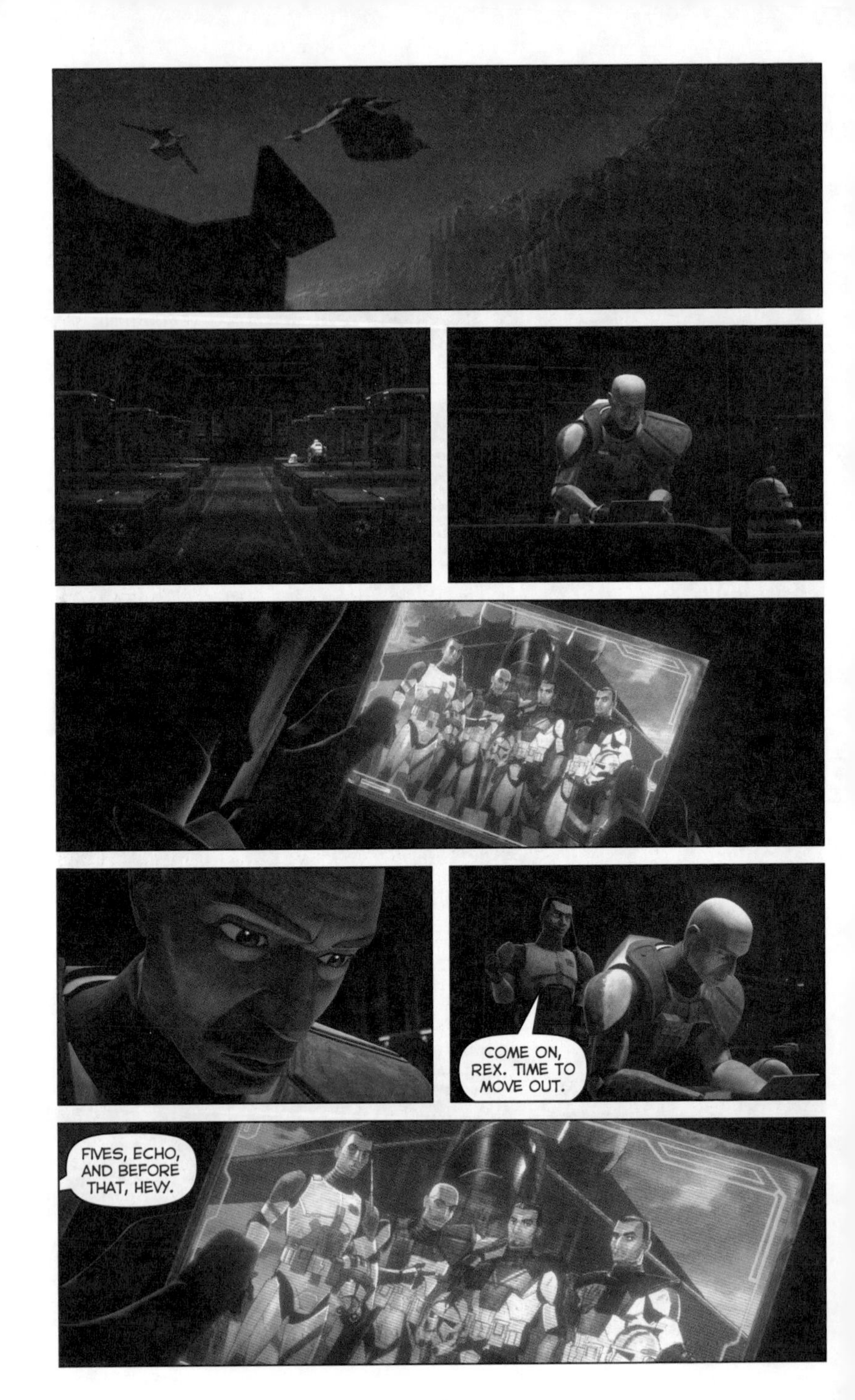
COME ON, REX. TIME TO MOVE OUT.
FIVES, ECHO, AND BEFORE THAT, HEVY.

THERE'S SO MANY TROOPERS...GONE.

YEAH, REGULAR FOLK DON'T UNDERSTAND. SOMETIMES IN WAR, IT'S HARD TO BE THE ONE THAT SURVIVES.

THAT'S WHAT I'M WORRIED ABOUT.

WELL, WHAT DO YOU MEAN?

I DIDN'T TELL THE GENERALS. THEY MIGHT THINK I'M CRAZY. IN FACT, YOU MIGHT THINK I'M CRAZY.

WHAT IS IT?

I THINK ECHO'S ALIVE.

THAT'S NOT POSSIBLE. HE DIED AT THE CITADEL.

THE WAY THE DROIDS ARE COUNTERING US HERE, THE STRATEGIES I'M USING, THEY'RE ALL OLD BATTLE PLANS ECHO AND I DREW UP TOGETHER.

LOOK, REX, I HEAR WHAT YOU'RE SAYING. BUT IT'S JUST NOT POSSIBLE.

I HOPE YOU'RE RIGHT. BUT THE FACT IS, ECHO'S FINGERPRINTS ARE ALL OVER THESE SEPARATIST STRATEGIES.

REX. YOU HAVE TO ADMIT WHAT YOU'RE SAYING IS A LONG SHOT AT BEST, AND MOST LIKELY, MISPLACED HOPE. I NEED YOU TO BE FOCUSED ON THIS.

I--I KNOW, I KNOW. DON'T WORRY.

SO, WHAT SQUAD ARE WE TAKING IN?

CLONE FORCE 99.

I'VE HEARD MIXED THINGS ABOUT THESE GUYS.
THEY HAVE A 100 PERCENT SUCCESS RATE.

IT'S NOT THAT THEY WIN--IT'S HOW THEY WIN THAT WORRIES ME.

ALL GROUND CREW: WE HAVE A SHUTTLE COMING IN HOT ON PLATFORM TT-3-9-7. CLEAR THE AREA.

REPEAT, COMING IN HOT ON PLATFORM TT-3-9-7.

SO WHY HAVEN'T I HEARD OF THIS SQUAD?

EXPERIMENTAL UNIT CLONE FORCE 99. THEY'RE DEFECTIVE CLONES WITH, UH... DESIRABLE MUTATIONS.

99, EH? NICE TOUCH.

THEY CALL THEMSELVES "THE BAD BATCH."

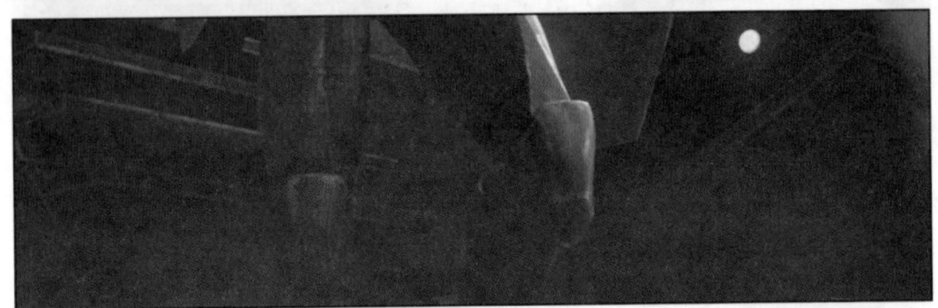

THE CAVALRY HAS ARRIVED!

THESE GUYS ARE CLONES? THEY DON'T LOOK LIKE CLONES TO ME.

SERGEANT, GOOD TO SEE YOU AGAIN.
YOU TOO, SIR.

THIS IS HUNTER.

SORRY WE'RE LATE, COMMANDER.
WE WERE PUTTING DOWN AN INSURRECTION ON YALBEC PRIME WHEN YOUR COMM CAME IN. HAD A FEW UNFORESEEN...COMPLICATIONS.

HAHAHA! EVER FOUGHT A MALE YALBEC?

UM, NO. CAN'T SAY I HAVE.

YOU'RE LUCKY. ONLY WAY TO KILL 'EM IS WITH ONE OF THESE.

THAT'S RIGHT. WRECKER HERE CUT OFF THE QUEEN'S STINGER WHILE SHE WAS STILL ALIVE.
THAT'S WHY ALL THOSE YALBEC MALES TRIED TO EAT US.

UH, TECHNICALLY, THEY WERE TRYING TO MATE WITH US.
AND, FOR YOUR INFORMATION, THE STINGER OF A YALBEC QUEEN IS A DELICACY ON SOME PLANETS.

THEY CALL HIM TECH.

YEAH, HE CAN FILL YOUR HEAD WITH USELESS INFO FOR HOURS.

CROSSHAIR, ON THE OTHER HAND, HE'S NOT MUCH OF A CONVERSATIONALIST...

BUT WHEN YOU HAVE TO HIT A PRECISE TARGET FROM TEN KLICKS, CROSSHAIR'S YOUR MAN.

SO, COMMANDER, WHAT KIND OF "SUICIDE MISSION" DO YOU HAVE FOR US THIS TIME?

LET'S GET GOING. WE'LL BRIEF YOU ON THE WAY.

WHAT ARE YOU LOOKING AT?

WE DON'T USUALLY WORK WITH "REGS."

"REGS"?

HE'S TALKING ABOUT REGULAR CLONES. BUT DON'T TAKE IT PERSONAL.

WE'RE ALL ON THE SAME TEAM, SO CUT THE ATTITUDE AND LISTEN UP. HERE'S THE MISSION.

OUR TARGET IS THIS CYBER CENTER. IT'S THE "BRAINS" OF THE ENTIRE SEPARATIST CAMPAIGN HERE ON ANAXES.

I COULD DEMOLISH THAT WITH ONE HAND! YEAH!

THIS ISN'T A DEMO JOB, WRECKER. IT'S STRICTLY A RETRIEVAL OPERATION.

SECTOR ONE, ALERT. ENEMY GUNSHIP APPROACHING YOUR LOCATION. COME IN, SECTOR ONE.

ROGER, ROGER.

FIRE!

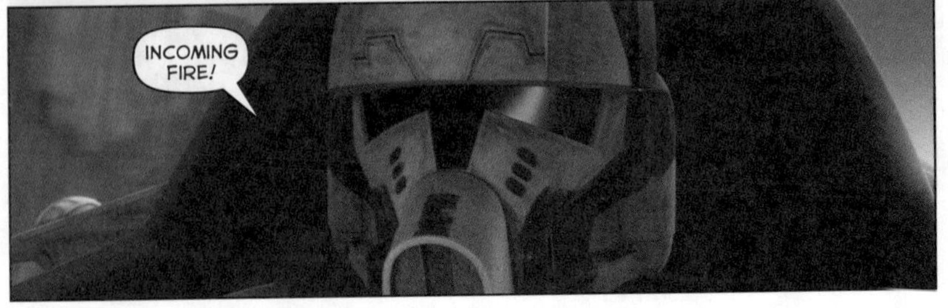
INCOMING FIRE!

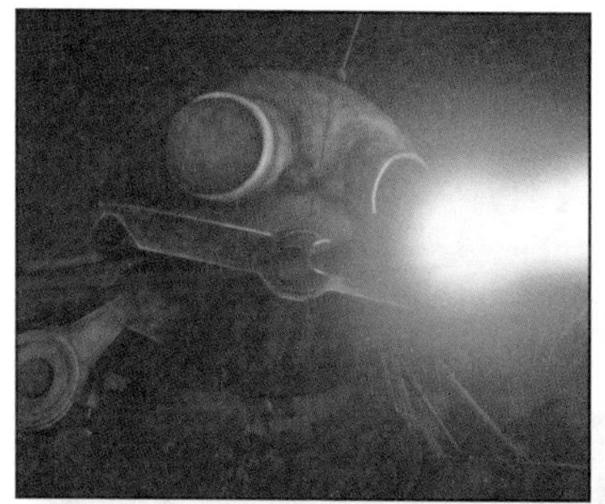

WE'RE GOING DOWN! HAHAHAHA!

SCREECH

WE ALWAYS GET SHOT DOWN WHEN WE TRAVEL WITH REGS.

CODY!
HELP! HE'S TRAPPED!

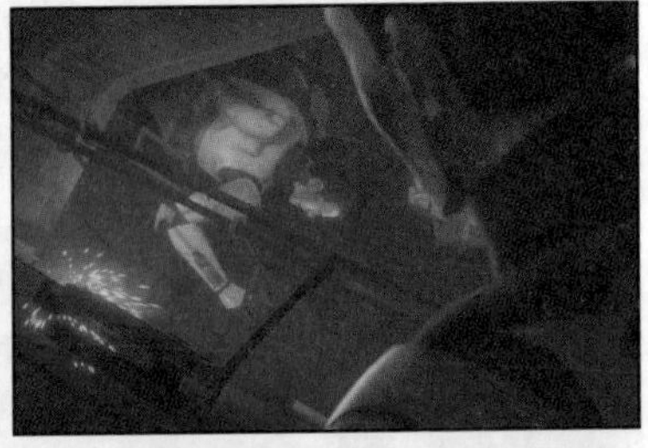

WE HAVE TO DO SOMETHING. I'LL GET HIM.

WHOA, WHOA, WHOA, WHOA, WHOA. EASY, CAPTAIN.

WRECKER, GET HIM OUT.

GET BACK!

THIS IS RIDICULOUS! HE'S GONNA NEED HELP TO GET CODY OUT OF THERE.

HE'S GONNA GET THE GUNSHIP OUT OF THERE. NOT CODY.

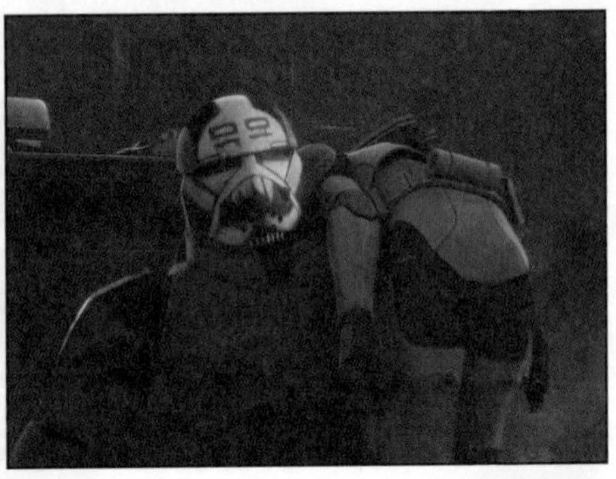

BOOM

UGH!

HE HAS
INTERNAL DAMAGE.
I CAN CUT THE PAIN.
BUT HE NEEDS HELP
FAST.

WE ALL NEED HELP.

THAT BLAST
GAVE AWAY OUR
POSITION.

I THOUGHT
GETTING SHOT
DOWN GAVE AWAY
OUR POSITION.

EVERYONE, FIND COVER.
WE'LL HOLD THIS POSITION
AND LET THEM COME TO US.

I DON'T THINK SO, CAPTAIN. THAT'S NOT OUR STYLE. WE PREFER GOING TO THEM.

BAD BATCH! PLAN 82, "SHOCKWAVE"!

LET'S GET TO WORK.

BLAST THEM!

FOOM

PTANG

45. MARK 151.

45. MARK 151.

ZZZT

75. MARK 357.
75. MARK 357.
WHAT THE...

FZZZZT

SPIDER DROIDS. FAN OUT!

KABOOM

ANY MORE? COME ON!

THAT WAS SOME SHOW YOU PUT ON JUST NOW.

JUST DOING OUR JOB, CAPTAIN.

HEY, LOOK, CROSSHAIR, THIS LITTLE CLANKER LIKES YOU. HAHAHA!

GROW UP, WRECKER.

WE SHOULD MOVE OUT BEFORE REINFORCEMENTS ARRIVE. OUR POSITION HAS BEEN COMPROMISED.

WE WANTED TO SPEAK TO YOU DIRECTLY, SIR. THIS INFILTRATION IS IRREGULAR.

WERE THERE JEDI WITH THIS SQUAD?

JUST CLONES. BUT USING TACTICS LIKE WE HAVE NEVER SEEN BEFORE.

INTERESTING. THEY'RE ON FOOT NOW, IN THE MIDDLE OF NOWHERE. SWEEP THE AREA, LOCATE THESE CLONES, AND NOTIFY ME IF THE INCURSION ESCALATES.

SO, I GET WHAT MAKES THE OTHER BATCHERS UNIQUE, BUT WHAT'S SO SPECIAL ABOUT HUNTER?

HE CAN PUT UP WITH THE OTHER THREE.

HE WAS ENGINEERED WITH HEIGHTENED SENSES. A PLACE LIKE THE CYBER CENTER, HUNTER CAN FEEL THE ELECTROMAGNETIC FREQUENCIES FROM ANYWHERE ON THE PLANET.

AND HERE I THOUGHT WE WERE SMART JUST USING A HOLOMAP.

WELL, MAPS CAN BE WRONG. HUNTER NEVER IS.

AGHH! AGH!
HANG IN THERE, CODY.

LISTEN UP. WE HAVE TO MOVE OUT.

COMMANDER CODY'S IN NO POSITION TO MOVE.

ALREADY CALLED IN EVAC. KIX WILL STAY WITH CODY UNTIL IT ARRIVES. I'M IN CHARGE NOW.

AND I'VE GOT A PLAN TO GET INTO THAT CYBER CENTER.

IF YOUR PLANS ARE SO GOOD, WHY DID COMMANDER CODY HAVE TO CALL US IN?

YOU CAN'T TALK TO CAPTAIN REX LIKE THAT!
SAYS WHO?

WHOA!

PUT HIM DOWN!

STAY OUT OF IT.

HEY! WATCH IT!
UH, GUYS, COME ON.

WRECKER, DROP HIM. NOW.

AW.

FELLAS, COME ON!

WE'RE ALL FIGHTING FOR THE SAME THING, RIGHT?

ALL RIGHT THEN. LET'S CUT THE CHATTER AND FINISH WHAT WE STARTED. WE'LL DO IT YOUR WAY, CAPTAIN. FOR COMMANDER CODY.

OKAY. LET'S GEAR UP AND MOVE OUT.

NOT OUR PRIMARY TARGET. IT'S AN OUTPOST. SHOULD WE TAKE IT?

PROBABLY EASIER THAN GOING AROUND.
ALL RIGHT, WHAT ARE YOUR ORDERS?
WE PICK THEM OFF FROM THE TREE LINE ONE BY ONE?

ACTUALLY, I WAS THINKING WE'D TAKE A PAGE FROM YOUR BOOK. RUSH THEM HEAD-ON.
I LIKE YOUR STYLE.

KAFOOM

BLAM

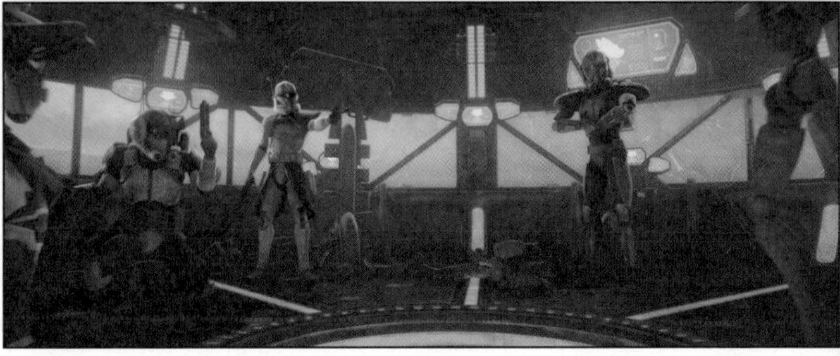

IS IT OVER ALREADY? AW, MAN!

NOT BAD. FOR A REG.

ALL RIGHT, THERE IT IS. THE CYBER CENTER.

IT LOOKS LIKE THE CYBER CENTER ITSELF HAS MINIMAL GUARDS, ABOUT THIRTY DROIDS.

OH...WAIT. WAIT! I GOT A MASSIVE SIGNAL COMING IN. A WHOLE PLATOON OF DROIDS IS HEADED THIS WAY.

SOMEONE'S NOTICED OUR HANDIWORK BACK AT THE CRASH SITE.

YEAH. MAKE SURE YOU KEEP AN EYE ON THOSE INCOMING SEPARATIST FORCES.
I WANT TO KNOW WHEN THEY REACH THIS OUTPOST.
YOU GOT IT, CAP.
WE'VE GOTTA MOVE SWIFTLY.

WE'LL GRAB SOME SPEEDER BIKES AND FLANK THEM FROM THE BACK.

DO YOU KNOW WHAT'S GOING ON?
MAYBE IT'S ANOTHER DRILL--

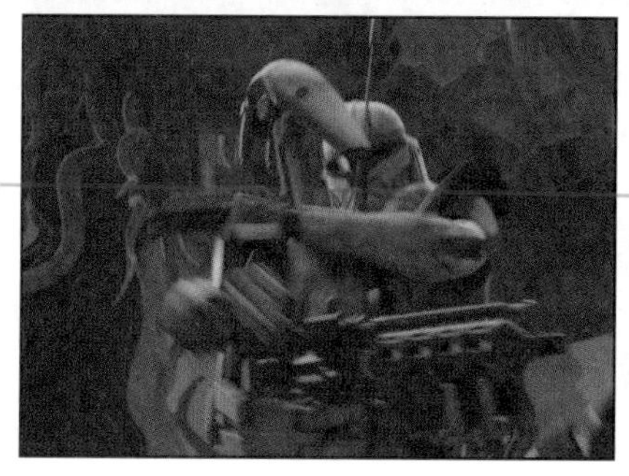

IS EVERYONE IN POSITION?

AFFIRMATIVE.

AFFIRMATIVE.

CAP, YOU WANTED TO KNOW WHEN THOSE SEPARATIST FORCES BREACHED THE OUTPOST.

WELL, THEY'RE GETTING THERE JUST ABOUT NOW.

SIR, WE TRACKED THE CLONE STRIKE TEAM HERE. THEY SEEM TO HAVE CAPTURED THIS LOCATION AND DESERTED IT.

I CANNOT CALCULATE THE LOGIC OF THIS ASSAULT.

THERE IS NO TACTICAL ADVANTAGE TO TAKING THE OUTPOST.
THEIR TARGET WILL BE THE NEARBY CYBER CENTER. THEY MUST KNOW ABOUT THE ALGORITHM.

GET ME IN CONTACT WITH THE CYBER CENTER AT ONCE!

PUT ALL DROIDS ON ALERT. AN ATTACK IS COMING.

AN ATTACK IS COMING? WHEN--

BLAM

KAFOOM

ALL UNITS TO THE FRONT DOOR!

HMM. THIS IS A DELICATE OPERATION.

WHAM

BOOM! YOU TAKE TOO LONG.

WE'RE IN.

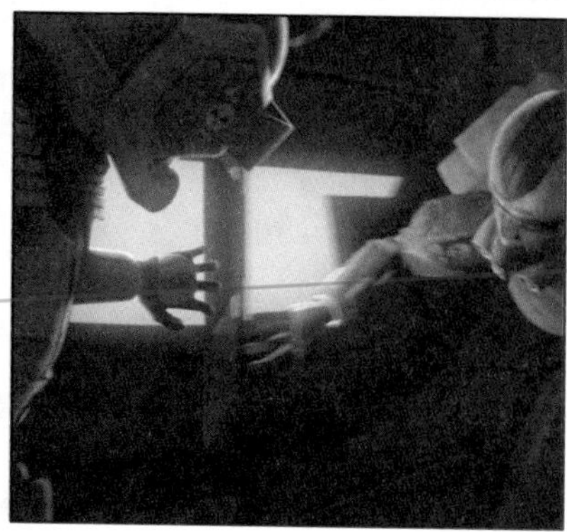

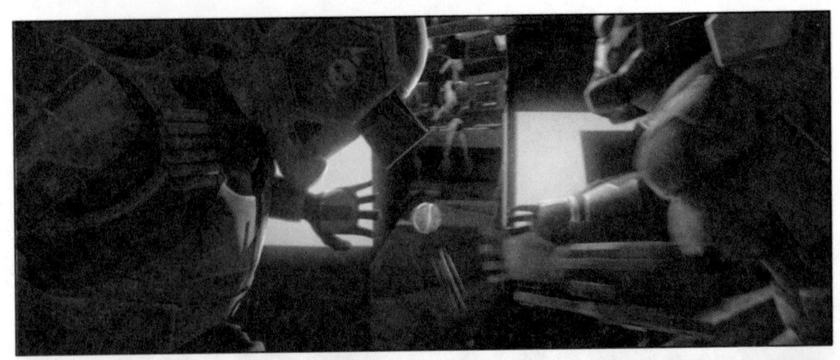

ZZZZZT

ZZT

TECH, GET TO WORK ON THESE COMPUTERS. WE'LL GO GET THE REGS.

ZZZT

FZZT

HEY, WHERE DID YOU COME FRO--

WHAT TOOK YOU SO LONG, WRECKER?
HEY, THIS IS A "DELICATE OPERATION."

BETTER GET IN THERE, CAP.

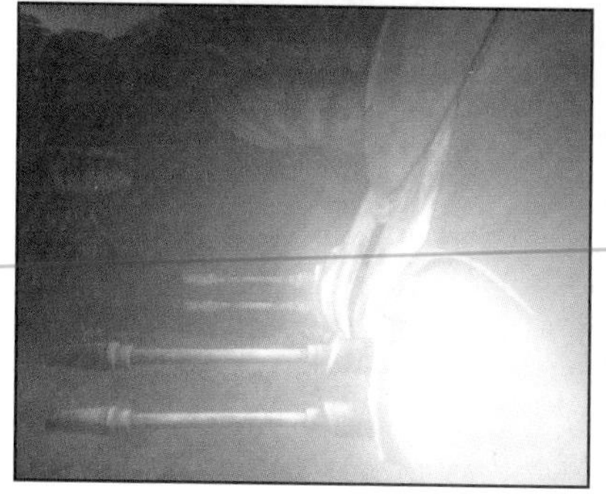

OKAY, I'M IN. WHAT AM I LOOKING FOR?

HERE'S THE ALGORITHM. YOU'RE LOOKING FOR A PROGRAM USING THIS SEQUENCE.

FOUND IT. THIS IS STRANGE. IT'S NOT A PROGRAM.

IT'S A LIVE SIGNAL FROM ANOTHER PLANET...

SKAKO MINOR.

A LIVE SIGNAL?

CROSSHAIR, WE'RE GONNA NEED A LIFT.

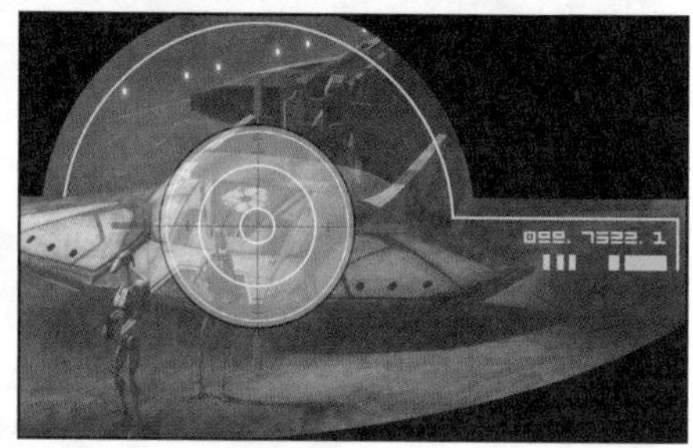

NOT GONNA BE A PROBLEM.

HERE IT IS. THIS IS AUDIBLE.

PATCH ME IN. I WANT TO HEAR IT.

GRR GRR

WHAT IS THAT? IT SOUNDS ALMOST... ALMOST HUMAN.

IT CAN'T BE.

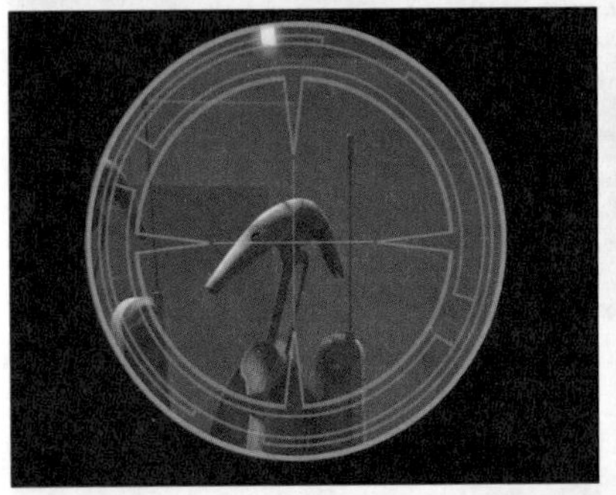

KABLAM

WE GOTTA GO! NOW!

TECH, FIND OUT WHO'S SENDING THAT SIGNAL. ASK WHO THAT IS.

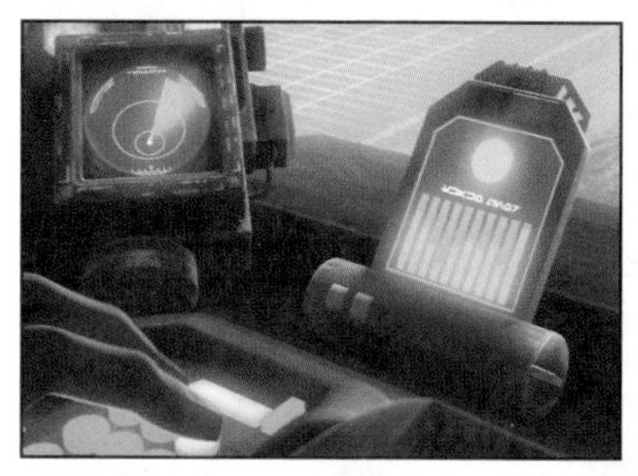

CT-1409. CT-1409.

I... I DON'T BELIEVE IT.

WE'RE GONE. REX, LET'S GO.

REX, NOW!

PTHEW

WE HAVE CHASED THE CLONES OUT OF THE CENTER, SIR. THEY ARE RETREATING BACK TOWARD REPUBLIC LINES.

DID THEY DOWNLOAD ANYTHING FROM THE CENTRAL COMPUTER?

THERE SEEMS TO BE NO INTEL MISSING. BUT THERE APPEARS TO HAVE BEEN A CONNECTION MADE WITH SKAKO MINOR.

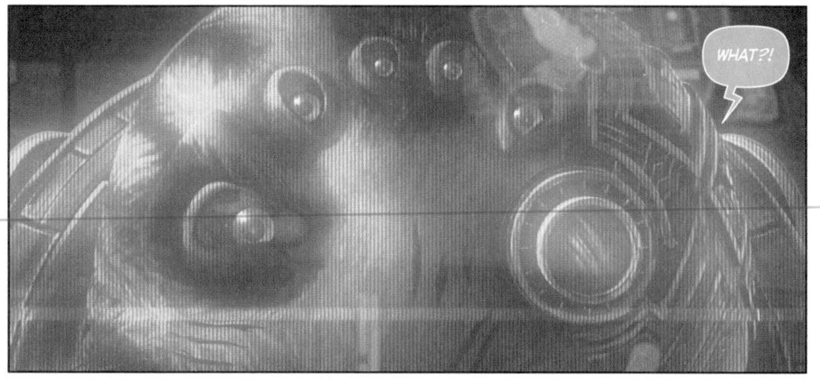
WHAT?!

THAT NUMBER, CAP, WHAT DID IT MEAN?

CT-1409... THAT WAS ECHO'S NUMBER. HE'S ALIVE.

EPISODE 2

A DISTANT ECHO

The search for truth begins
with belief.

CONSPIRACY!

AFTER REPEATED SETBACKS ON THE PLANET ANAXES, AN ELITE CLONE SQUAD IS DEPLOYED TO INVESTIGATE THE SEPARATISTS' TACTICAL ADVANTAGE.

THIS SPECIAL UNIT, CALLED THE BAD BATCH, INFILTRATES ADMIRAL TRENCH'S CYBER CENTER TO STEAL...

...A STRATEGIC ALGORITHM CAPABLE OF PREDICTING THE REPUBLIC'S EVERY MOVE.

WHAT OUR HEROES FOUND WAS A LIVE SIGNAL FROM THE ARC TROOPER KNOWN AS ECHO...

...A CLONE LONG BELIEVED TO BE DEAD.

WORD IS THE GENERAL STAFF ISN'T COMPLETELY BEHIND THIS MISSION.

I ADMIT THE IDEA THAT ECHO IS STILL ALIVE IS A LONG SHOT.

I'M SURE THE COUNCIL WILL APPROVE THE MISSION.
JUST REMEMBER THE PRIMARY GOAL IS TO LEARN HOW THE SEPARATISTS ARE PREDICTING OUR STRATEGY, WHETHER IT'S ECHO BEHIND IT OR NOT.

WELL, IF YOU WANT MY OPINION, IT SOUNDS LIKE A TRAP. BUT ME AND THE BOYS WILL TAG ALONG ANYWAY, IF ONLY TO SAY "I TOLD YOU SO."

JUST MAKE SURE YOU'RE READY IF WE GET THE GO-AHEAD FROM GENERAL KENOBI.

IF YOU'RE CERTAIN HE'LL APPROVE THE MISSION, WHY WAIT? LET'S GET GOING.

FIRST, WE HAVE THAT THING TO DO.
UH, WHAT THING?

YOU KNOW.

WE DON'T HAVE TIME FOR THAT, SIR.

YES, WE DO.

WELL, I'LL JUST LET YOU TWO SORT THIS OUT. I'LL BE WAITING ON THE SHIP WITH THE REST OF THE TEAM.

COME ON, REX. I'M LATE AS IT IS.

YOU'RE LATE AGAIN.

PADMÉ, I'M SO SORRY. WE DIDN'T ANTICIPATE THE OUTER RIM SIEGES WOULD LAST THIS LONG.

THAT WOULD BE WHY THEY CALL IT A SIEGE, ANAKIN.

I KNOW, I JUST THOUGHT THAT I--
YOU THOUGHT YOU COULD BRING A SWIFT END TO THE CONFLICT SINGLE-HANDEDLY.

YEAH.
HEH. ANAKIN, WHAT YOU'RE DOING IS IMPORTANT. THE REPUBLIC NEEDS YOU ON THE FRONT LINES JUST AS THEY NEED MY VOICE IN THE SENATE.

I KNOW.

OH, GREAT.

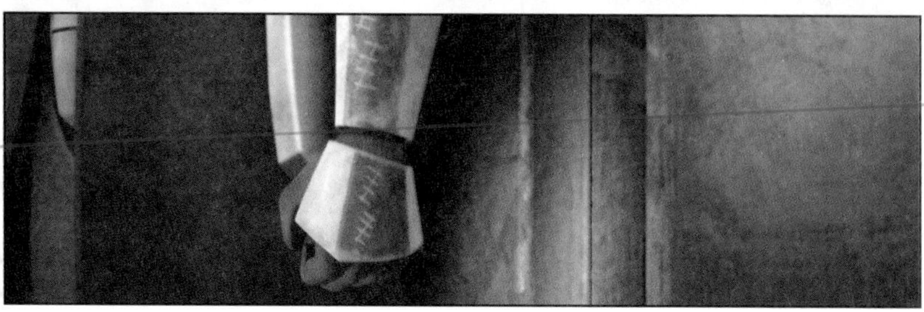

BANG
BANG
WHAT IS IT?

OBI-WAN IS COMING.
NO, THAT'S NOT IT. THERE'S SOMETHING ELSE.

IT'S REX. I'M WORRIED HE'S LETTING HIS PERSONAL FEELINGS DRIVE HIM TOO MUCH ON THIS MISSION.

I WONDER WHERE HE LEARNED THAT.

REX, WHERE'S ANAKIN? I NEED TO SPEAK TO HIM ABOUT THIS MISSION.
WELL, GENERAL, HE'S, UM...
WELL, HE'S INSIDE YOUR BARRACKS, ISN'T HE?
YES, SIR.

WHAT'S GOING ON HERE?

NOTHING, SIR. I WAS JUST WAITING FOR THE GENERAL... UH, GENERAL.

YOU'LL HAVE TO DO BETTER THAN THAT, CAPTAIN.

YOU'VE KNOWN REX A LONG TIME. WHEN YOU THROW CAUTION TO THE WIND AND TAKE CHANCES, WHERE IS HE?

RIGHT BESIDE ME.

THEN MAYBE THAT'S WHERE YOU SHOULD BE FOR HIM, ANI. TRUST HIS INSTINCTS LIKE HE TRUSTS YOURS.

I'M JUST TRYING TO LOOK OUT FOR HIM.

I KNOW YOU ARE.

I LOVE YOU, ANI.
I LOVE YOU TOO.

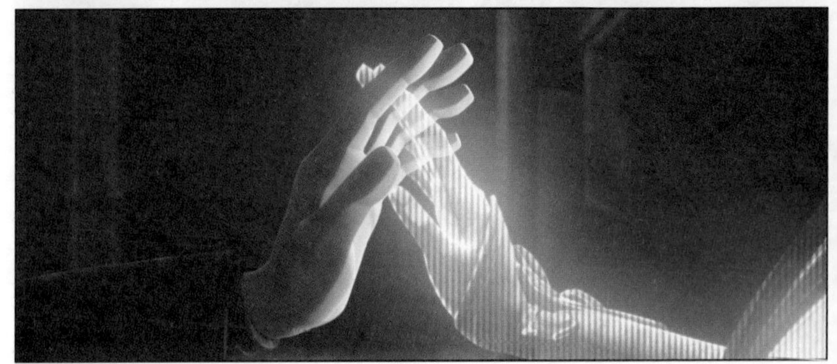

THEN WHAT IS ANAKIN DOING IN THERE?

AH, HE'S SPOT-CHECKING MY GEAR, SIR.

REALLY? WITHOUT YOU?

WELL...

HERE YOU GO, REX. AND TRY NOT TO BREAK IT AGAIN.

ANAKIN. ABOUT THIS MISSION, THE COUNCIL THINKS--

THAT IT'S A GOOD IDEA? I AGREE. LET'S GET MOVING, REX.

NO, WAIT. THAT'S NOT--
NO TIME.

I HOPE YOU AT LEAST TOLD PADMÉ I SAID HELLO.

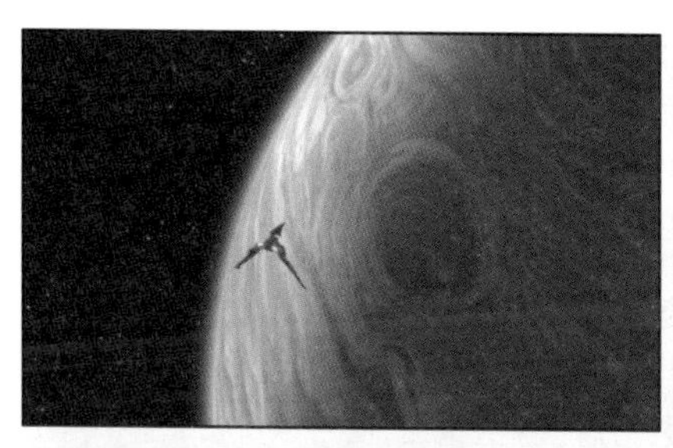

SO, HOW MANY MISSIONS HAS YOUR TEAM BEEN ON, SERGEANT?

HONESTLY, SIR, I'VE LOST COUNT. ALL THE ACTION SORT OF BLURS TOGETHER.

I KNOW YOU WORK WITH CODY SOMETIMES, BUT WHO DO YOU GUYS REPORT TO?

HMM...GOOD QUESTION. CAN'T SAY I'VE GOT AN ANSWER.

YEAH!

WE ARE APPROACHING SKAKO MINOR. IT LOOKS TO BE A DIFFICULT LANDING.

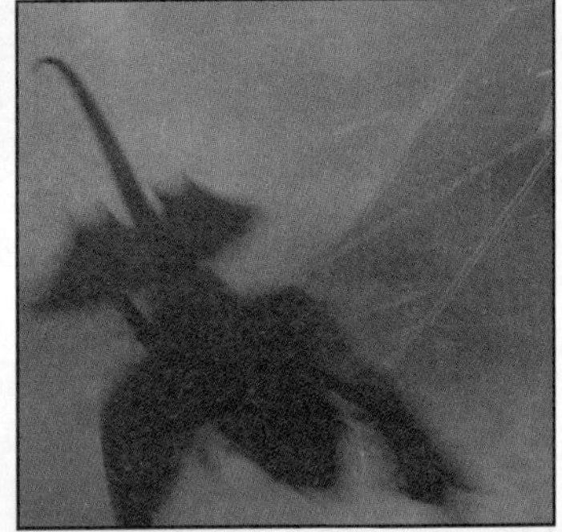

REX, WHAT DO WE KNOW ABOUT THIS PLACE?

ON THIS PART OF SKAKO, THERE'S A RACE OF LOCALS, THE POLETECS. ALL WE KNOW IS THEY'RE VERY PRIMITIVE.

"PRIMITIVE" IS BEING KIND. MY INTEL SAYS THE POLETECS WORSHIP FLYING REPTILES.

FRWAP

OH! WHAT THE HECK WAS THAT?

IT'S ONE OF THOSE REPTILES.

I WANT THAT THING OFF MY SHIP.

HOLD ON! HOLD ON! DON'T JUST RUN OUT THERE.

HEY! GET OFF OF THERE!

HEY, CALM DOWN. WE NEED TO TALK TO THEM.

WHY?

THE GENERAL'S RIGHT.

WATCH OUT, REX!

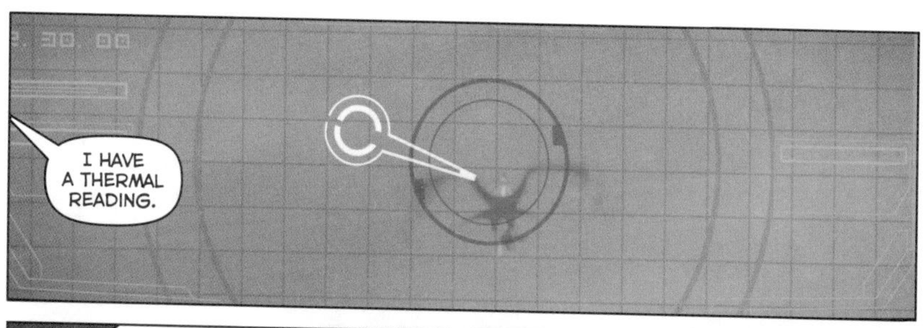
I HAVE A THERMAL READING.

POINT-TWO-FIVE EAST, ELEVATION 175.

RELAX. I'LL HANDLE THIS.

THOOOM

WHAT ARE YOU DOING?

GOING FOR A RIDE.

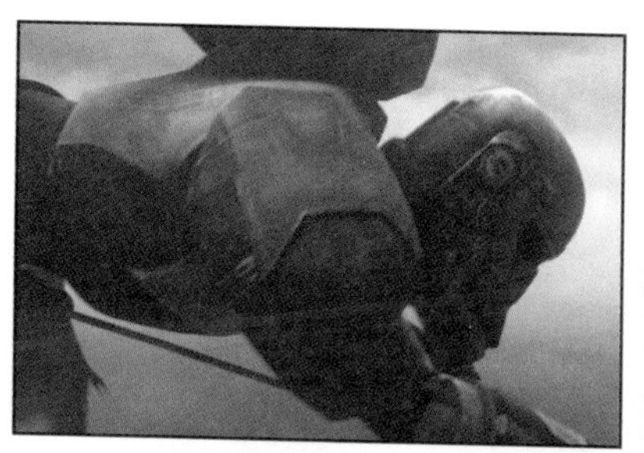

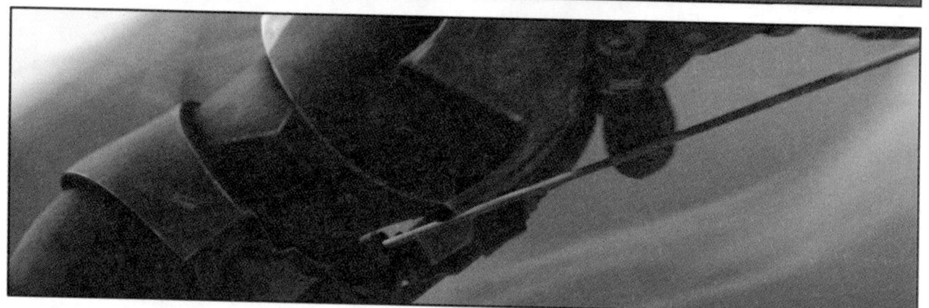

TECH, I'M WITH THE GENERAL. HONE IN ON MY SIGNAL.

BO LUA FES DALEEN.

O DEE GIRO ME FES DABA.

OKAY, I THINK WE'RE GONNA HAVE A SLIGHT COMMUNICATION PROBLEM HERE.

WO SOO DEBA SA FELVOO.

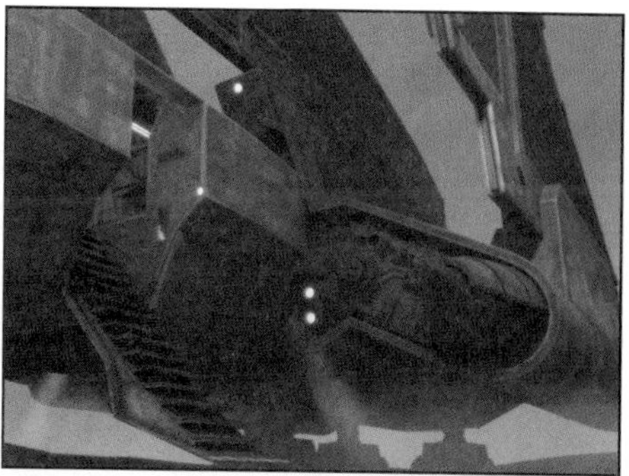

THAT CREATURE STILL HAS A HOLD OF THE GENERAL.

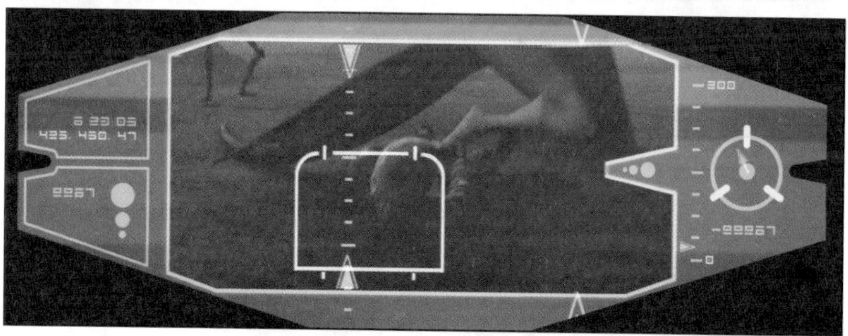
200
6 23 03
423. 450. 47
2267
-22667
0

WE'RE GOING IN, BUT REMEMBER WHAT THE GENERAL SAID. "NO CASUALTIES, DISARM ONLY."
WE'RE ON IT, CAPTAIN.
WRECKER, CROSSHAIR, ROCKSLIDE!

FE DAS GELOO, DAS FEDO.

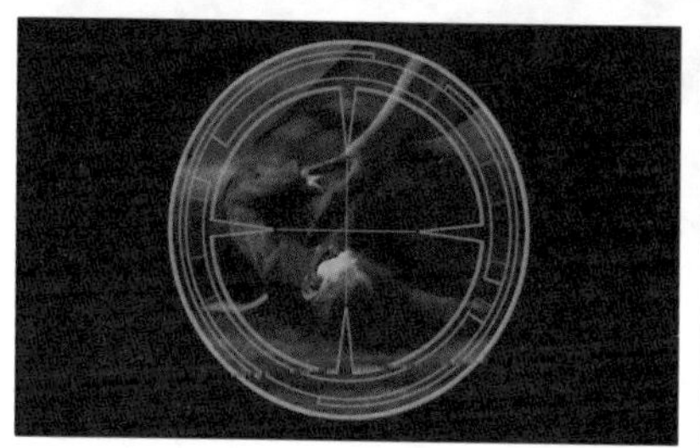
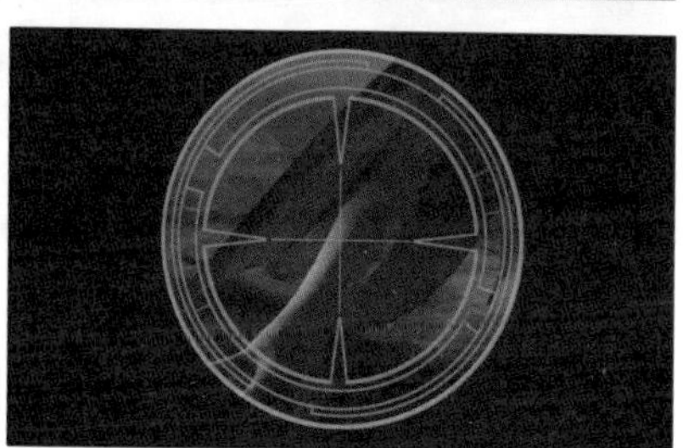

FWUMP
ZZZZT

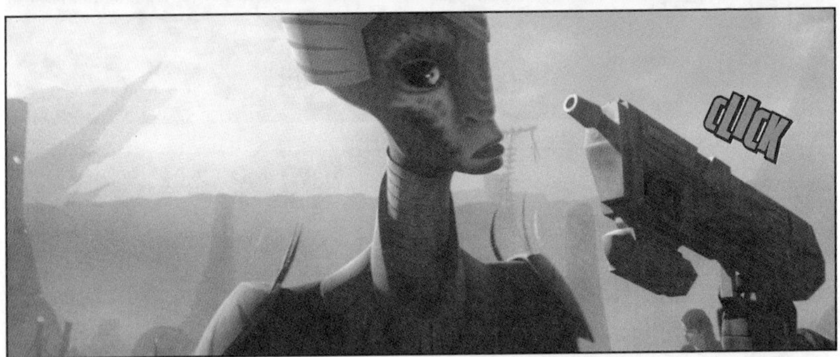
CLICK

ZEE MA FALTEE SFWAO.

TECH, TRANSLATE WHAT HE SAID.

HE SAYS HE DOES NOT WANT OUR WAR ON HIS PLANET. THAT IS WHY HE TOOK OUR LEADER.

WE DIDN'T BRING THE WAR HERE. IT WAS WAT TAMBOR AND THE SEPARATISTS.

DASNY JAN FYNAD SNEDA. TUMOOK TAMBOR AYSO...SEPARATISTS.

TELL HIM WE APOLOGIZE FOR WHAT'S HAPPENED. BUT TELL HIM THE ENEMY IS HOLDING ONE OF OUR MEN PRISONER IN PURKOLL.
AS SOON AS WE RESCUE HIM, WE'LL LEAVE HIS PLANET FOR GOOD.

FYNAD SNEDA JOOR KUPPA DNASY ERNKLNASD. N ER ERE TUMOOK SNEDA FYNA. ANS DNASY FYNAD. SIN SU.

GAN DWEDESA NASO FRENDA TOOBARO. ERRON DAMSTE FREEMA BONDO.

THE CHIEF SAYS HE WILL PROVIDE US WITH SCOUTS AND LEAD US TO TAMBOR'S CITY. FROM THERE, WE'RE ON OUR OWN.

ANY HELP IS BETTER THAN NO HELP.

WE ARE RECEIVING A TRANSMISSION FROM ADMIRAL TRENCH ON ANAXES.

PUT HIM THROUGH.

PARDON THE INTRUSION, MINISTER TAMBOR...BUT I HAVE DISTURBING NEWS.

YOU MAY PROCEED, ADMIRAL.

AN INFILTRATION TEAM OF CLONES HAS TRACED THE ALGORITHM SIGNAL TO SKAKO. I BELIEVE YOUR OPERATION THERE IS IN JEOPARDY.

THE REPUBLIC WOULD NOT DARE ATTACK US. THE TECHNO UNION HAS CORPORATE NEUTRALITY.

FROM WHAT I HAVE SEEN, THAT WOULD NOT MATTER TO THESE REPUBLIC OPERATIVES.

THEN WE SHALL BE READY FOR THEM.

MADA FORKULL.

HOPE NOBODY'S SCARED OF HEIGHTS.

WELL, I'M NOT SCARED OF NOTHING. I JUST...WHEN I'M UP REAL HIGH, I GOT A PROBLEM WITH GRAVITY.

SPEAKING OF PROBLEMS, I AM NO LONGER PICKING UP ECHO'S SIGNAL.

I...I DON'T UNDERSTAND. YOU SAID IT WAS COMING FROM THIS CITY.

I CAN ONLY SPECULATE, BUT IT IS POSSIBLE THERE'S A LATENCY ISSUE WITH THE FREQUENCY CAUSED BY ALL THESE ATMOSPHERIC DISTURBANCES.

OR... MAYBE THEY SENT THE SIGNAL TO LURE US INTO A TRAP.
AND MAYBE YOUR FRIEND'S ACTUALLY DEAD.
WELL, I CAN'T BE THE ONLY ONE THINKING OF THAT.

LOOK, EVERY MISSION COULD BE A TRAP. THIS ONE IS NO DIFFERENT.
I'M TELLING YOU THAT SIGNAL IS BEING SENT BY ECHO HIMSELF! HE'S ALIVE!

I THINK YOU'RE LETTING YOUR PERSONAL FEELINGS GET IN THE WAY BECAUSE YOU LEFT HIM FOR DEAD AT THE CITADEL.

I HAD NO CHOICE. YOU HEAR ME?

OH, I DON'T BLAME YOU. I WOULD'VE LEFT HIM FOR DEAD TOO. BESIDES, HE'S JUST ANOTHER REG.

KARPOW

HEY!

WHY DON'T YOU
PICK ON SOMEONE
NOT YOUR SIZE?

YOU'LL BE A WHOLE
LOT SMALLER WHEN I'M
THROUGH WITH YOU.

THAT'S
ENOUGH!

SERGEANT, TAKE YOUR
MEN AND SCOUT THE AREA FOR
A TOWER ENTRANCE.

I WANT
TO TALK TO
MY CAPTAIN
ALONE.

REX, I HATE TO SAY IT, BUT...YOU HAVE TO PREPARE YOURSELF FOR THE POSSIBILITY THAT ECHO IS DEAD, AND THIS IS ALL A SEPARATIST TRICK.

SIR, I HAVE WATCHED SO MANY OF MY BROTHERS FALL DURING THIS WAR, AND I TRY NOT TO HANG ON TO ANY ONE OF THEM.

BUT THAT CHANGED WHEN I HEARD THAT SEPARATIST TRANSMISSION. IT WAS NO ALGORITHM. THAT WAS ECHO'S VOICE. I KNOW IT.

I HOPE YOU'RE RIGHT. BUT IF, FOR SOME REASON, YOU'RE WRONG...

THEN I'LL DEAL WITH IT.

CRASH

WE'RE IN BUSINESS, GENERAL. TECH REGAINED ECHO'S SIGNAL. IT'S COMING FROM THIS TOWER. HOW'S IT GOING, TECH?

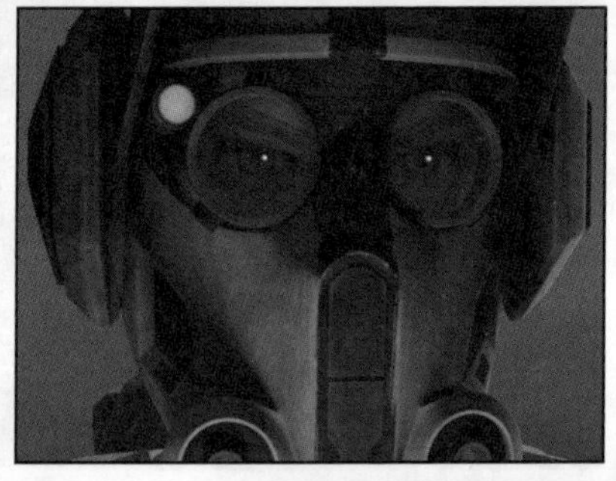

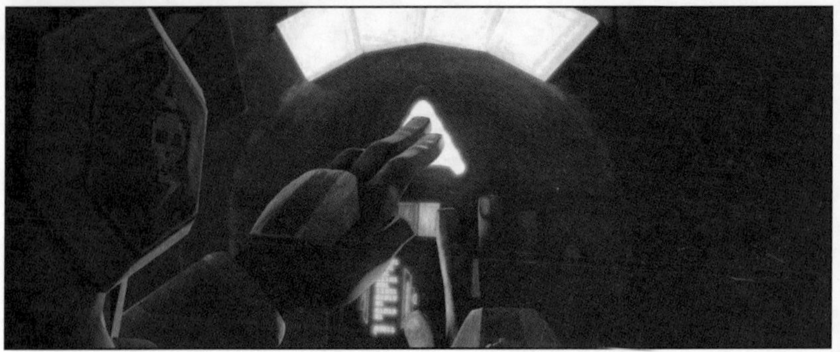

SORRY IT TOOK SO LONG.

HEY, CROSSHAIR, CHECK IT OUT.

YEAH, IT'S A LIFT.

WELL, WE ALREADY KNEW THAT.

WAIT, WAIT, WAIT. A LIFT? HOW FAR UP ARE WE GOING?
DON'T WORRY, WRECKER. I'LL HOLD YOUR HAND.
HEY! CUT IT OUT, SARGE. JUST GIVE ME SOME DROIDS TO CRUSH.

REMEMBER, THIS IS A STEALTH MISSION. NO BLASTING, NO BLOWING THINGS UP. NOBODY KNOWS WE'RE HERE.

ARGHHH!

INTRUDERS! ATTACK!

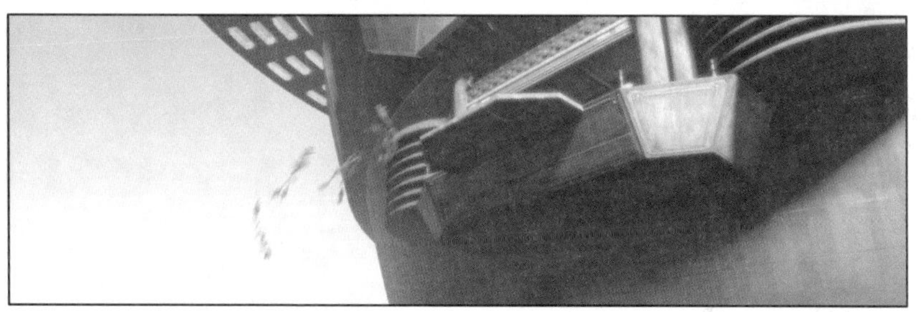

RATATATAT

SO MUCH FOR STEALTH.

KAFOOM

YEAH! HAHA! HA-HA! YEAH!

UH... SORRY. I JUST GOT EXCITED.

I'VE STILL GOT A LOCK ON ECHO'S SIGNAL.

ALL RIGHT, MEN. LET'S HUNT SOME DROIDS.

NOW YOU'RE TALKING! YEAH!

KABLAM

BLAM

WHERE EXACTLY IS ECHO'S SIGNAL COMING FROM?

STRANGE. I JUST LOST THE SIGNAL.
WHAT? HOW CAN THAT BE? THERE'S NO "ATMOSPHERIC DISTURBANCES" UP HERE.

WELL, I HAVE A NEW THEORY. I'M SURPRISED I DID NOT CONSIDER IT EARLIER.
THE SIGNAL IS ONLY TRACEABLE DURING DATA TRANSMISSIONS.
SO UNTIL ECHO DISPENSES MORE INTEL, I CANNOT PICK UP THE SIGNAL.

OKAY, WE'RE SPLITTING UP. SEARCH EVERY DOOR.
IF SOMEONE FINDS ECHO, CONTACT THE OTHERS. WE GO IN TOGETHER JUST IN CASE THERE'S TROUBLE.

DROP YOUR WEAPON! YOU ARE SURROUNDED!

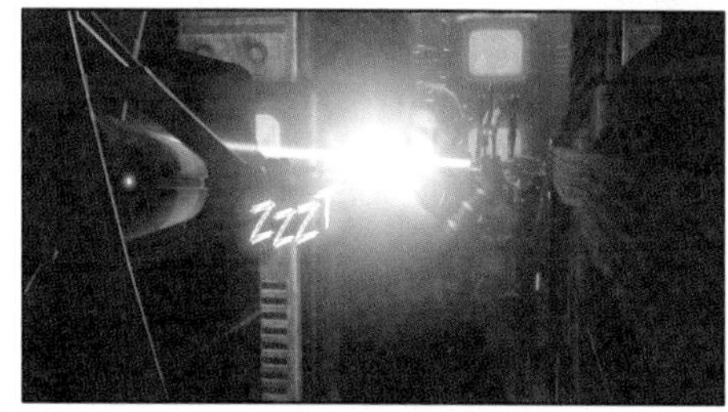
ZZZT

AH! IT APPEARS THE SIGNAL IS BACK. IT'S FROM UP AHEAD.

IN THERE.
KABLAM

TECH, OPEN THIS DOOR.

YOU CLONES ARE SO PREDICTABLE.

WAT TAMBOR.

YOUR ALGORITHM PREDICTED NEARLY EVERY MOVE YOU MADE TO INFILTRATE PURKOLL.

THERE IS NO ALGORITHM. WE KNOW YOU'RE HOLDING A PRISONER OF WAR HERE.

PRISONER? I DON'T KNOW WHAT YOU MEAN, CAPTAIN.

I AM LEAVING HERE WITH MY FRIEND.

YOUR FRIEND IS DEAD. HIS MIND IS OURS.

LIAR!

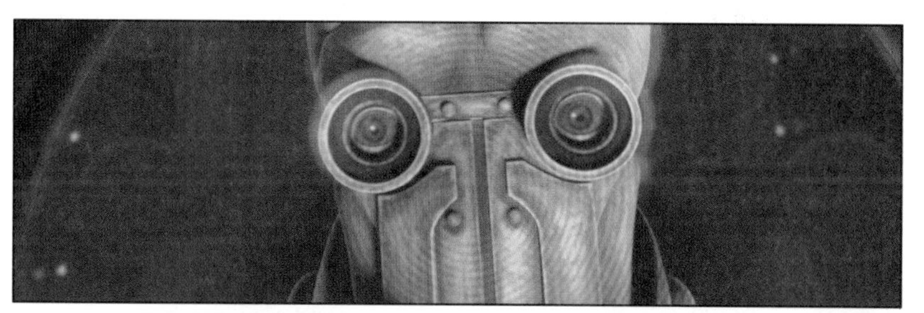

ZZZT

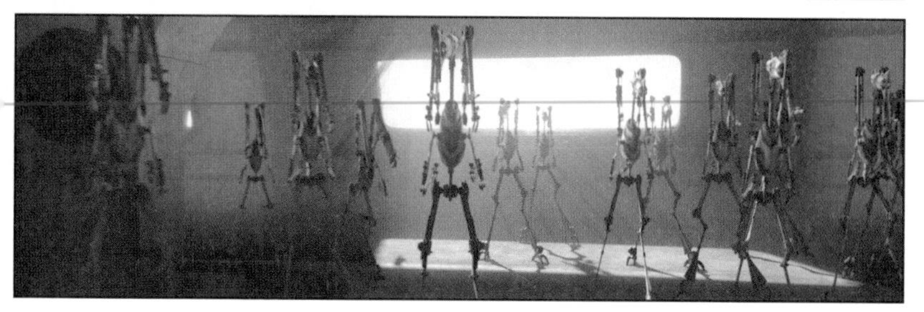

TZKT

TECH, OPEN THAT DOOR FOR REX!
YES, SIR!

I HOPE YOU FIND WHAT YOU'RE LOOKING FOR, CAPTAIN.

I DON'T LIKE THE LOOK OF THIS.

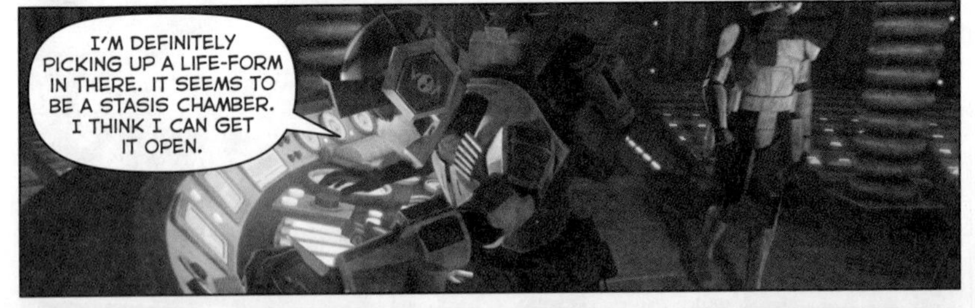
I'M DEFINITELY PICKING UP A LIFE-FORM IN THERE. IT SEEMS TO BE A STASIS CHAMBER. I THINK I CAN GET IT OPEN.

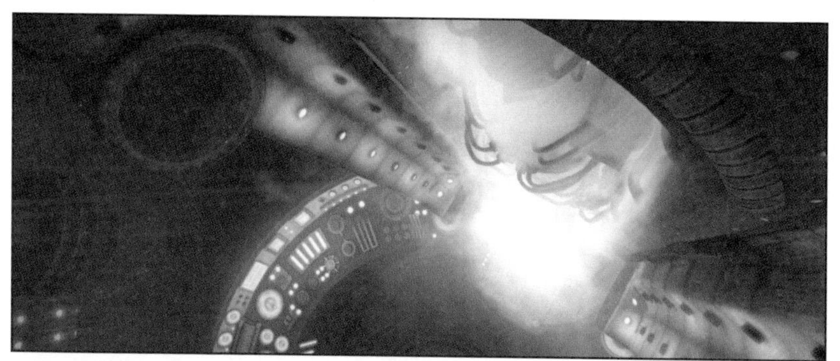

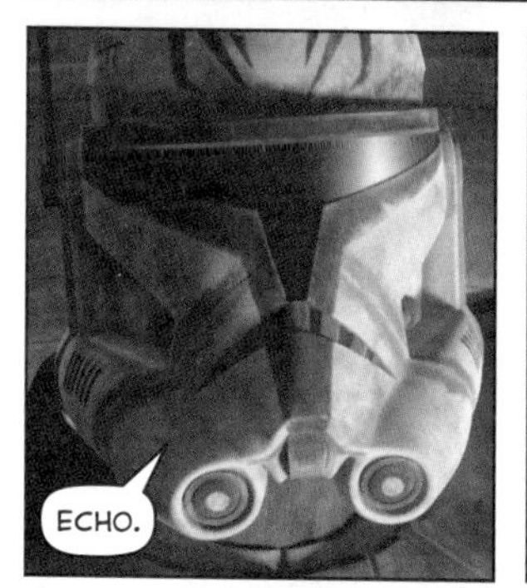
ECHO.

TECH. WE GOT TO GET HIM OUT OF HERE. FIGURE OUT HOW TO UNPLUG HIM FROM-- FROM THIS MESS.

WHAT HAVE THEY DONE TO YOU?

WE--WE HAVE TO GET TO THE SHUTTLE TO ESCAPE THE CITADEL. NO! I'LL GO FIRST.

ECHO.
NO! NO. NO.
ECHO, IT'S REX. I'M HERE.

REX? YOU, YOU CAME BACK FOR ME.

YES. YES, I DID.

WHAT? WHAT HAPPENED? WHERE AM I?

IT'S OKAY, ECHO. YOU'RE SAFE NOW. JUST SIT TIGHT, TROOPER. YOU'RE GOING HOME.

EPISODE 3

ON THE WINGS OF KEERADAKS

Survival is one step on the path to living.

TRAPPED!

ON AN UNSANCTIONED MISSION
TO RESCUE ARC TROOPER ECHO...

...GENERAL SKYWALKER, CAPTAIN REX, AND
THE BAD BATCH TRAVEL TO SKAKO MINOR...

...HEADQUARTERS OF
THE TECHNO UNION.

AFTER A HARROWING ENCOUNTER WITH THE NATIVES...

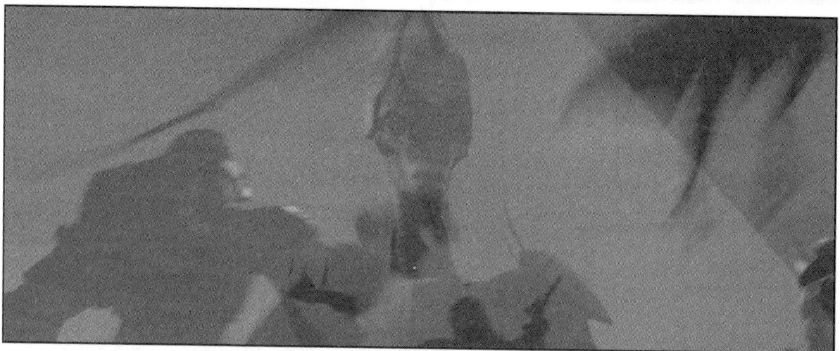

...OUR HEROES INFILTRATE THE CITY OF PURKOLL...

...ONLY TO FIND THEMSELVES SURROUNDED BY WAT TAMBOR'S FORCES.

HUNTER, HOLD THEM OFF. I'LL CHECK ON REX AND ECHO.

SITUATION'S ALMOST UNDER CONTROL OUT THERE. HOW'S IT GOING IN HERE?

I'M STILL TRYING TO DECRYPT ECHO'S CEREBRAL INTERFACE.
UNTIL I DO, WE CANNOT DISCONNECT HIM FROM THIS COMPUTER SYSTEM.

HOW IS HE, REX?

HE'S TOO WEAK TO WALK. VERY DISORIENTED. DOESN'T EVEN REMEMBER HOW HE GOT HERE.

HE REMEMBERS BEING AT THE CITADEL, BUT THAT'S ABOUT IT.

ANY WORD ON THE EXTRACTION SQUAD?

WE CALLED IT IN, BUT NO WORD BACK.

WELL, THAT'S NO SURPRISE. WE KNEW WHEN WE GOT INTO THIS WE'D BE ON OUR OWN.

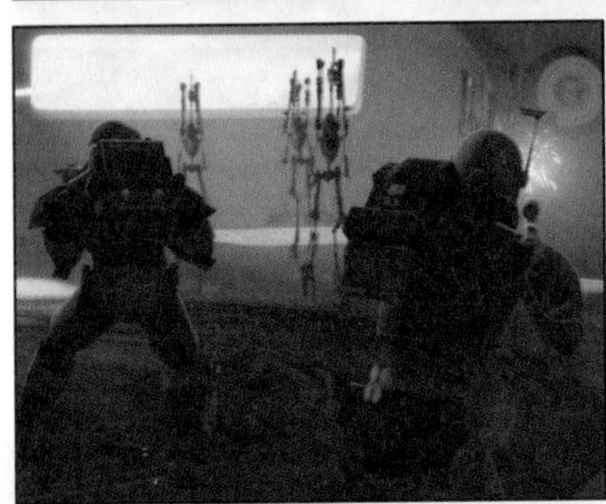

IT'S GONNA GET MORE DIFFICULT TO GET OUT OF HERE. THERE ARE SEVERAL SQUADS OF DROIDS CLOSING IN.

7 080.
5643. 8

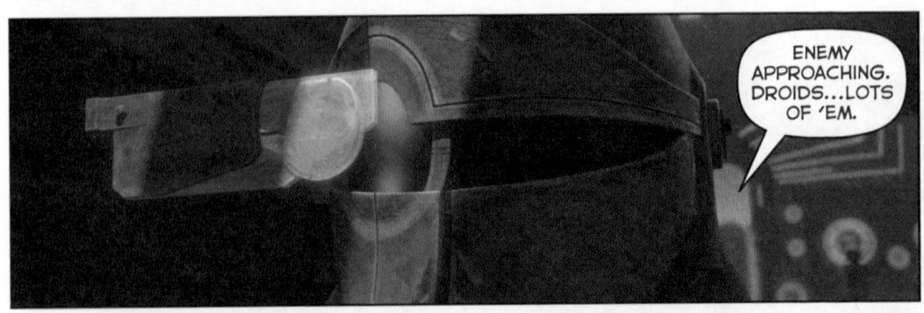
ENEMY APPROACHING. DROIDS...LOTS OF 'EM.

HOW LONG CAN YOU HOLD THEM OFF?

HOW LONG DO YOU NEED?

TECH, HOW MUCH LONGER?
NOT YET. I NEED MORE TIME.

WE HAVE THEM COMPLETELY SURROUNDED, SIR.
GOOD. SEND IN THE DECIMATOR.

FZZZT

I'VE GOT IT. WE CAN UNPLUG HIM NOW.

PSSSSHHHHH

PSSSSSHHHH

REX?

WHAT IS IT?

I GOT A BIG HEADACHE. HEH-HEH.

BETTER TO FEEL SOMETHING THAN NOTHING, OLD BUDDY.

IT'S A TOUCHING REUNION, GUYS, BUT WE NEED TO GET OUT OF HERE NOW.

THERE'S AN EXHAUST VENT THAT LEADS TO THE COOLING SYSTEMS RIGHT THERE.

ZZZZT

THEY'VE BREACHED THE FRONT DOOR. IT WON'T BE LONG BEFORE THEY'RE THROUGH THE SECOND.

THAT SHOULD GET IT OPEN.

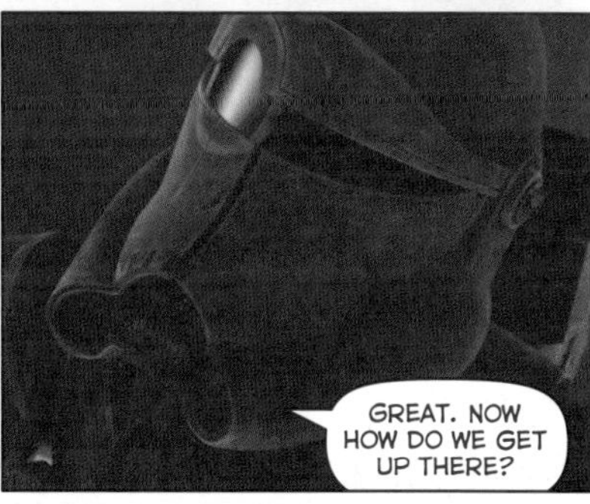
GREAT. NOW HOW DO WE GET UP THERE?

I CAN HELP WITH THAT.
WAIT, WHAT? WRECKER, WHAT ARE YOU DOING?

A HEADS-UP WOULD'VE BEEN NICE!

THE DOOR'S NEARLY BREACHED, SIR.

WHOA!

IT'S OKAY, WRECKER. I'VE GOT THIS.
WHAT ARE YOU DOING?

I'M PUTTING AN END TO TAMBOR'S LITTLE SCIENCE EXPERIMENT.

ARE YOU DONE? TIME'S UP.

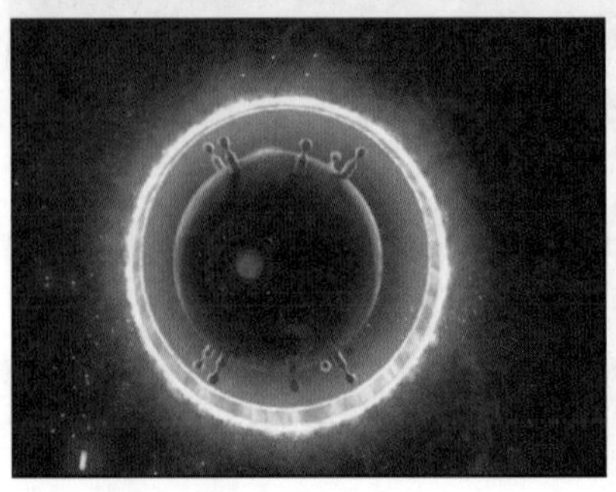

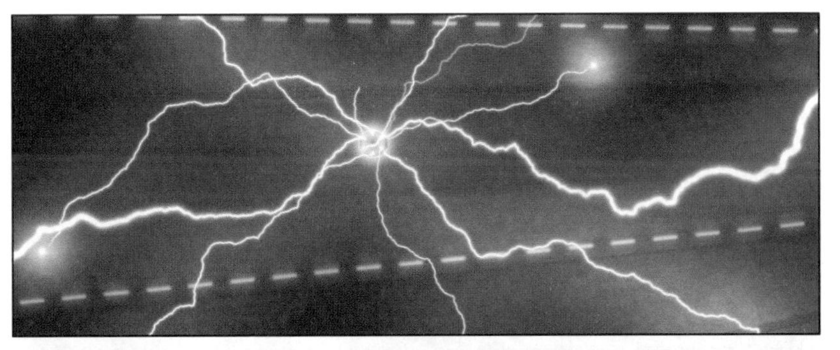

WHOA! WHOA! OH, NO! WHAT IS THAT THING? I DON'T LIKE IT! I DON'T LIKE IT!

IT'S TRYING TO GET ME! WHOA!

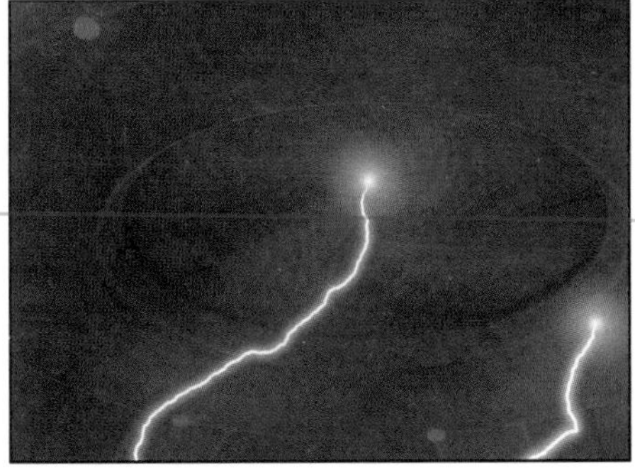

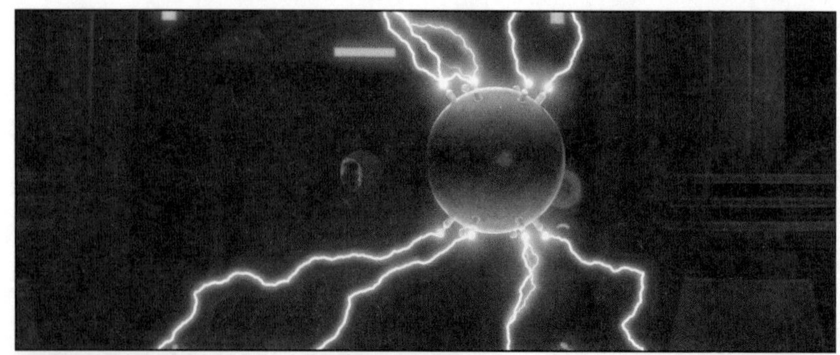

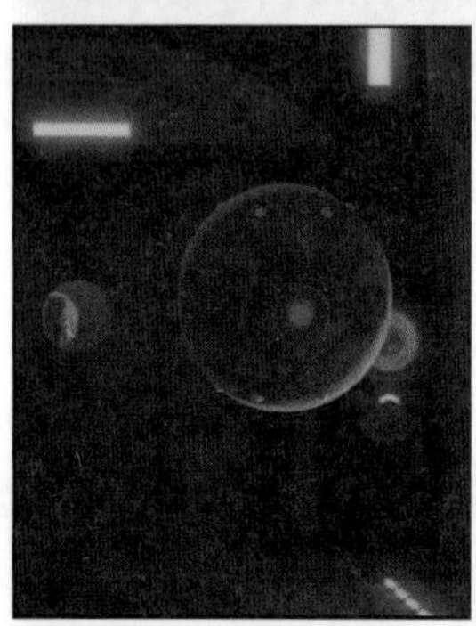

WHAT HAPPENED? WHY DID IT SHUT OFF?
NO ORGANIC TARGETS WERE DETECTED, SIR. THE ROOM APPEARS TO BE EMPTY.

OH, NO.

KABOOM

ORDERS, SIR?

THEY TOOK IT...TECHNO UNION PROPERTY! THEY'VE RUINED YEARS OF RESEARCH.

FIND THEM!

HUH. THIS VENTILATION CORRIDOR ACTS AS A COOLING SYSTEM FOR ALL THE COMPUTERS IN THE FACILITY.
HOW DID YOU KNOW IT WAS UP HERE, ECHO?

WELL, THEY GOT ACCESS TO MY MEMORY, AND I GOT ACCESS TO THE TECHNO UNION DATABASE.
ALL THEIR PLANS, INVENTORY, BUILDING SCHEMATICS... EVERYTHING.

YOU MEAN YOU CAN FIND US A SAFE WAY OUT OF HERE?
WELL, THERE IS A WAY, BUT YOU'RE NOT GONNA LIKE IT.

I DON'T KNOW ABOUT THIS.

I'M TELLING YOU, THERE'S A LANDING PAD ON THAT OTHER BUILDING.
SO YOU THINK THERE'S A SHIP THERE WE CAN STEAL?

WELL, I HOPE THERE'S A SHIP WE CAN STEAL.
LET'S HOPE THIS TRIP ISN'T FOR NOTHING.

OH, BOY. I CAN'T EVEN LOOK. JUST KEEP WALKING, TECH.
THAT'S FINE, BUT IF YOU FALL, DON'T TAKE ME WITH YOU.

UH-OH. I LOOKED. AHH! I THINK I'M GONNA BE SICK. NOT GONNA PANIC.

HANG ON, WRECKER. WE'RE ALMOST THERE.
GONNA BE OKAY. BREATHE.

TURN AROUND! GO BACK!

TSZKT

PTHEW

KABLAM

WHOA. WH-WHOA!

OH, BOY. GOTCHA!

ANYBODY GOT A BRILLIANT IDEA?

I DO HAVE A BRILLIANT IDEA.

I'M HANGING HERE!

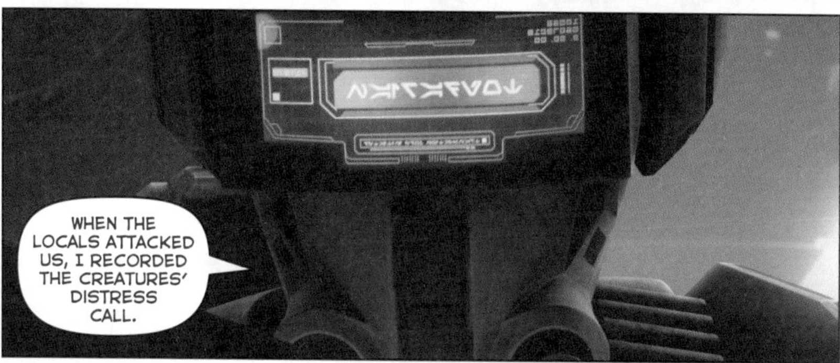
WHEN THE LOCALS ATTACKED US, I RECORDED THE CREATURES' DISTRESS CALL.

HE RECORDS EVERYTHING. IT'S A HOBBY.

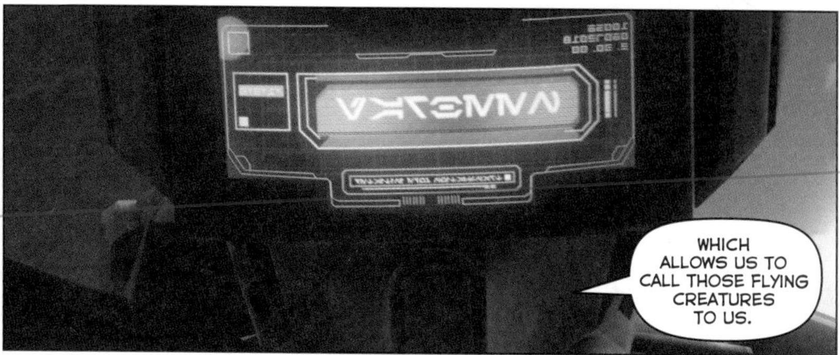
WHICH ALLOWS US TO CALL THOSE FLYING CREATURES TO US.

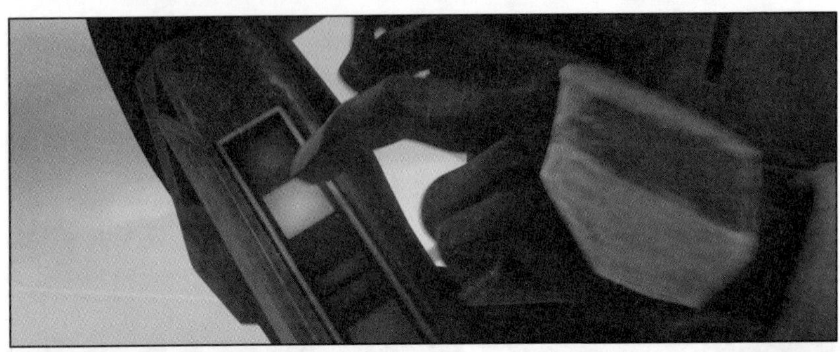

SCREEEE

OW! ENOUGH WITH THE SOUND! TAKE THAT!

KABLAM

THERE IS OUR RIDE OUT OF HERE!

NOW, HOW DO WE GET ON THEM?

HOW ELSE? WE JUMP!

ALL RIGHT, I'LL GO FIRST.

I DON'T WANNA DO THIS, BUT HERE I GO!

SEE YOU LATER!

UH, THAT WASN'T PART OF THE PLAN. THOSE THINGS CAN FLY!

WE HAVE TO SHAKE THOSE DROIDS! HOW DO I STEER THIS THING?

CRASH

HOW YOU HOLDING UP, ECHO?
NEVER BETTER, SIR! HAHA!

DYFAN NIDDI! DNASY FYNA ANAN!

THEIR LEADER IS IMPRESSED WE TAMED THE KEERADAKS, BUT HE WANTS TO KNOW WHY WE RETURNED HERE.

TELL HIM WE HAD NO CHOICE. TELL HIM...THAT WE WORE OUT OUR WELCOME IN PURKOLL.

NAH DISPIDI. DNICS FIN ASO KURUDI PURKOLL.

KABOOM

NOT GOOD. IF I KNOW TAMBOR, HE'LL COME AFTER US, AND THE POLETECS, WITH EVERYTHING HE'S GOT.

DYFAN NIDDI! DNASY FYNA ANAN!

WHAT'S HE SAYING, TECH?
HE SAYS THAT WE HAVE BROKEN OUR WORD. WE HAVE BROUGHT THE WAR TO HIS VILLAGE.

YOU'RE RIGHT. TELL HIM HE'S RIGHT, TECH.
TELL HIM WE DIDN'T PLAN TO DRAG HIS PEOPLE INTO WAR. BUT LOOK WHAT THE SEPARATISTS DID TO ONE OF OUR PEOPLE!

THEY TOOK AWAY HIS FREEDOM, HIS HUMANITY. THEY TRIED TO TURN HIM INTO A MACHINE.

DAJKH ADDI TOYN HEUJK. NAIDII JACOO PUI. DYFA NYNA ANAN.

THE TECHNO UNION CLAIMS IT'S NEUTRAL, BUT THEY HAVE CHOSEN SIDES. NOW YOUR PEOPLE HAVE TO CHOOSE.

COULDN'T HAVE SAID IT BETTER, REX.
UGH! LET'S HOPE IT WORKS, BECAUSE I SEE FORCES COMING...MORE THAN WE CAN HANDLE ALONE.

O PWANIR DEBRUIK PI NABROK.

REPORT.

THE CLONES ARE HIDING AMONG THE NATIVES.

TAKE THE REINFORCEMENTS AND BRING BACK MY EXPERIMENT.

UGGHH!

SMASH
ZZZZT

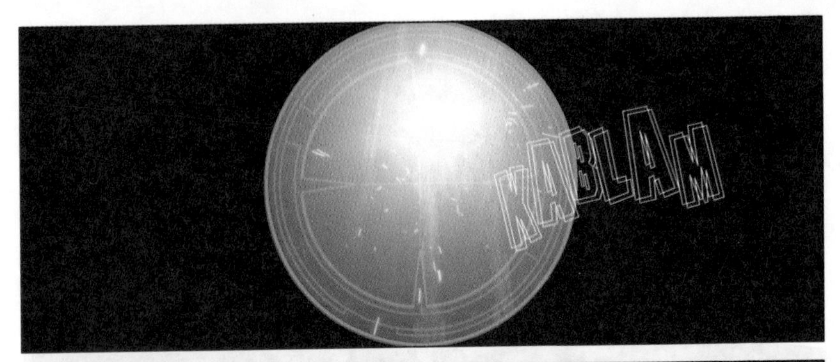
KABLAM

FZZZZ

KAFOOM

BOOM

Fzzzzz

REX, WE'VE GOTTA TAKE OUT THESE WALKERS. I'LL TAKE ONE. YOU TAKE THE OTHER.

DON'T WORRY, GENERAL. THE BOYS AND I CAN HANDLE IT. HUNTER, WRECKER, YOU'RE WITH ME.

STILL SHOWING OFF, HUH, GENERAL?

YOU KNOW ME, ECHO.

FZZZT

KSZZKT

FZZKT

THAT SEEMED TO WORK. BUT HOW DO WE GET UP THERE?

NO, NO. NOT AGAIN!

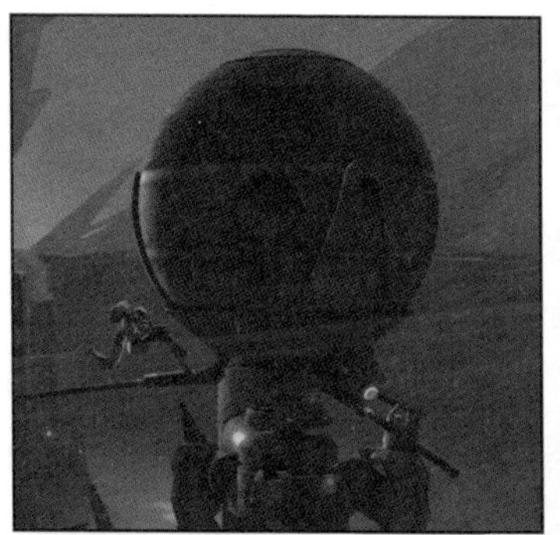

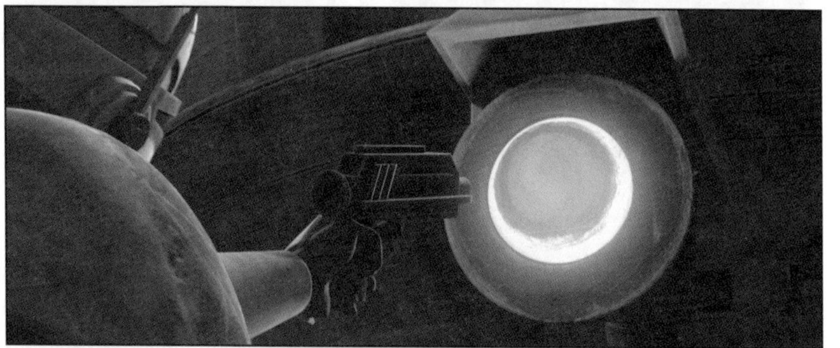

SMASH

SMASH

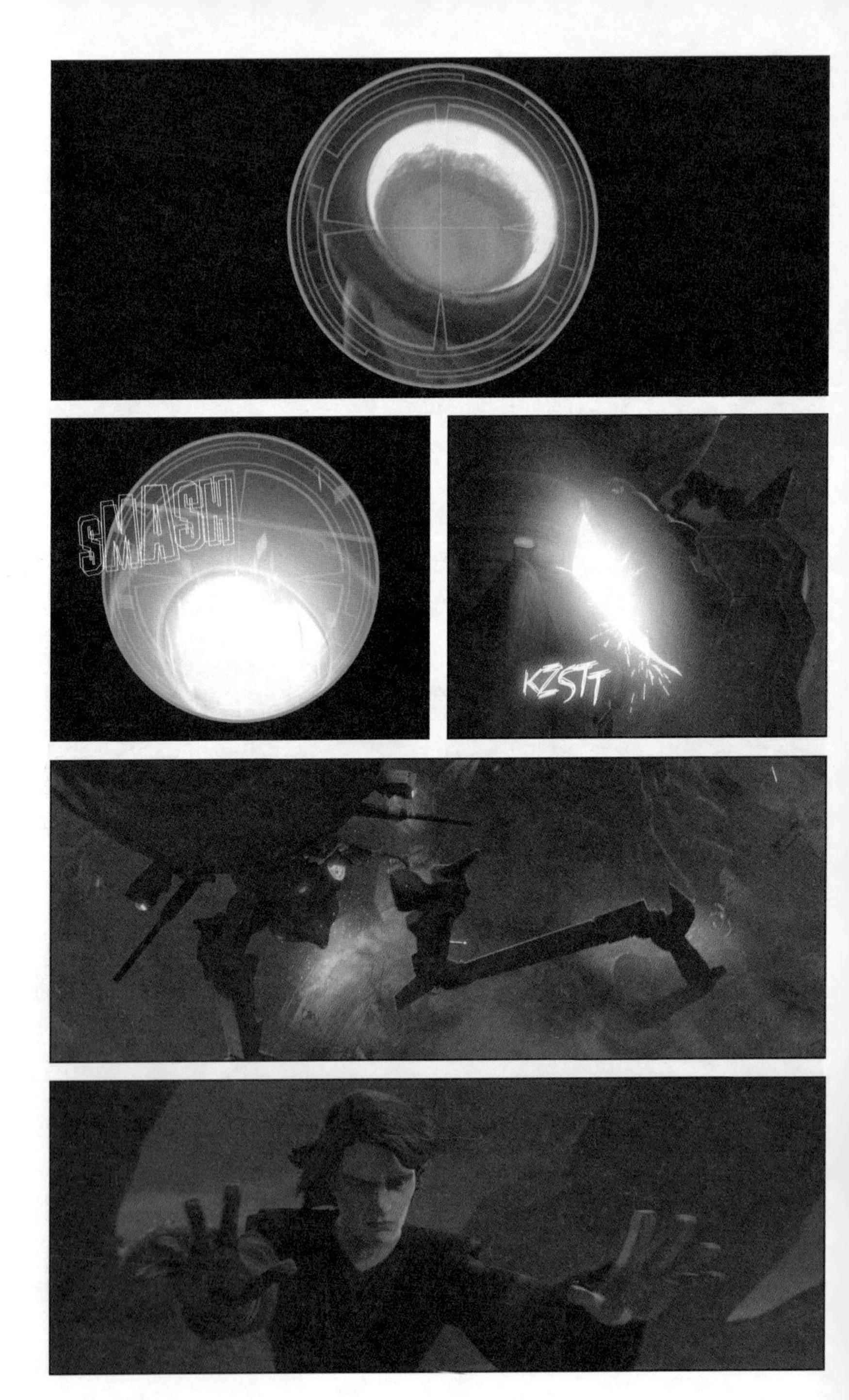
SMASH
KZSTT

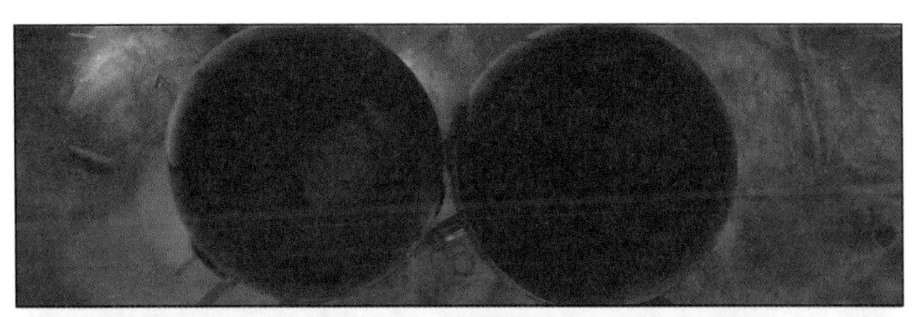

CRASH

IT'S HARD TO COMPETE WITH A JEDI.

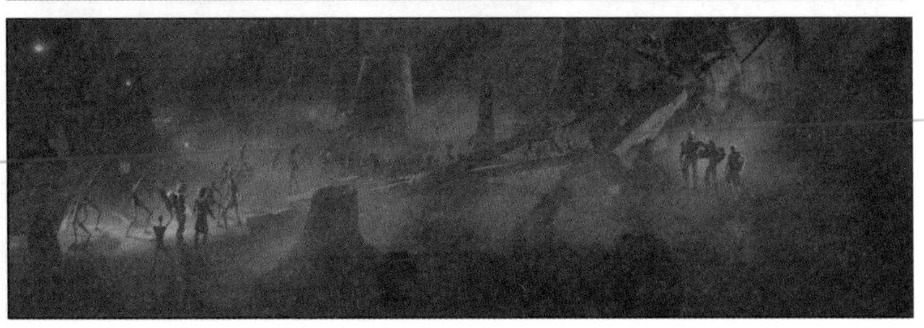

SIR, THE ATTACK FORCE HAS FAILED.

THE LOSS OF THE CLONE IS A DEVASTATING BLOW TO THE TECHNO UNION'S PROFIT MARGIN.

SHOULD WE INFORM THE SEPARATISTS OF OUR LOSS?

ALL IN GOOD TIME. WE MUST FIND A WAY TO RECOUP ON OUR INVESTMENT.

THANK YOU FOR HELPING US IN OUR FIGHT.

DANIV KUN TEP. ADDI TU.

DUN JEDI NEEK DNAS PUN KOOLA.

HE SAID THE JEDI WILL ALWAYS HAVE AN ALLY HERE ON SKAKO MINOR.

REX.
THANKS FOR
COMING AFTER
ME.

THAT'S WHAT
BROTHERS DO. I'M JUST
SORRY IT TOOK SO LONG.
HOPEFULLY, IT'S GONNA BE
JUST LIKE OLD TIMES.

YEAH.
JUST LIKE OLD
TIMES.

EPISODE 4
UNFINISHED BUSINESS

Trust placed in another
is trust earned.

REUNITED!

WITH THE HELP OF
THE BAD BATCH...

...CAPTAIN REX RESCUES HIS OLD FRIEND...

...ARC TROOPER
ECHO, FROM THE
TECHNO UNION.

THE SEPARATIST LOSS OF ECHO'S STRATEGIC ALGORITHM PROVIDES A CHANCE FOR THE REPUBLIC TO TURN THE TIDE IN THE BATTLE FOR ANAXES.

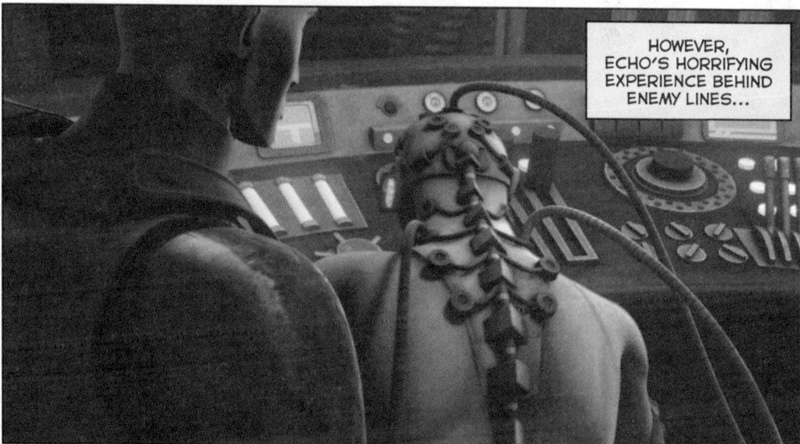
HOWEVER, ECHO'S HORRIFYING EXPERIENCE BEHIND ENEMY LINES...

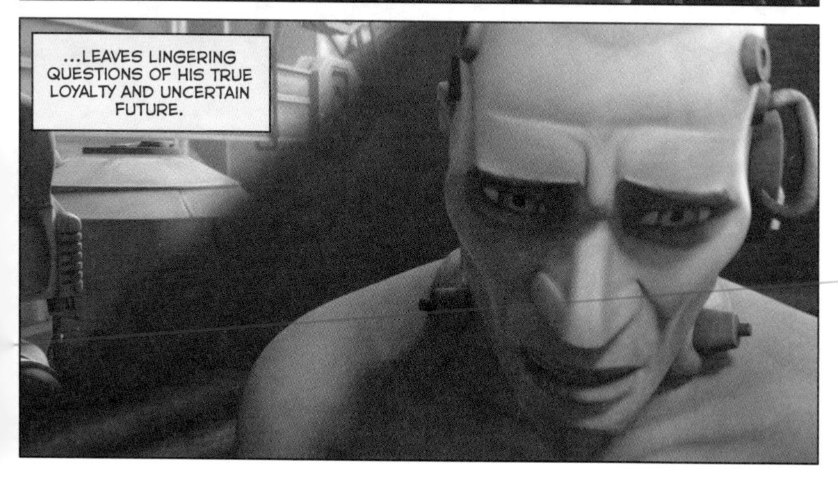
...LEAVES LINGERING QUESTIONS OF HIS TRUE LOYALTY AND UNCERTAIN FUTURE.

WE HAVE MORE THAN A DOZEN ACTIVE BATTLEFRONTS ON ANAXES, AND WE ARE LOSING NEARLY EVERY ONE.

BUT IF ADMIRAL TRENCH CAN NO LONGER ANTICIPATE OUR MOVES, WE NOW HAVE THE OPPORTUNITY TO RETAKE THE PLANET.

I CAN IMPROVE YOUR CHANCES.

UH, EXCUSE ME, GENERALS.

ECHO, I'M SORRY, BUT I JUST DON'T THINK YOU'RE READY FOR BATTLE YET.
I AM NOT A LIABILITY, REX.

I'M THE BEST CHANCE WE HAVE TO TAKE BACK ANAXES.

IF THE TROOPER HAS A PLAN, I'D LIKE TO HEAR IT.

MAY I?

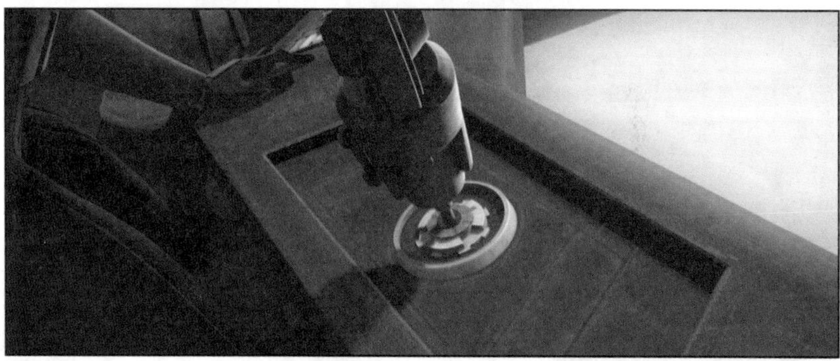

WHILE MASTER WINDU LEADS A TEAM TO RETAKE THE ASSEMBLY COMPLEX, THE BAD BATCH WILL ESCORT ME INTO TRENCH'S NEW COMM VAULT...

...WHICH, ACCORDING TO CURRENT INTEL, IS NOW LOCATED ON THIS SEPARATIST DREADNOUGHT ABOVE ANAXES.

ONCE I'M PLUGGED IN, I CAN FEED TRENCH STRATEGIES, BUT THIS TIME, YOU'LL KNOW EVERY MOVE BEFORE HE MAKES IT.

AND YOU ARE CERTAIN THAT IF WE GET YOU ON BOARD THAT SHIP, THAT YOU CAN CONVINCE TRENCH'S ARMY TO DO WHAT YOU WANT?

ABSOLUTELY. UNFORTUNATELY, I'VE BEEN DOING THIS FOR A WHILE, BUT THIS TIME I CAN HELP BRING ABOUT A REPUBLIC VICTORY INSTEAD OF A DEFEAT.

TECH, IS EVERYTHING READY?
YUP, SARGE. WE ARE READY.

STILL NOT SURE HOW WE'RE GONNA LAND ON THAT SHIP.
DON'T WORRY. ECHO SAYS HE'S GOT A PLAN.

THAT MAKES ME FEEL SO MUCH BETTER.
WHAT DO YOU MEAN BY THAT?
TO BE BLUNT, HIS MIND BELONGED TO THE SEPARATISTS UNTIL WE UNPLUGGED HIM. WE DON'T REALLY KNOW WHERE HIS LOYALTIES LIE.

YEAH. WELL, I KNOW. NOW, GET MOVING.

PLEASE TELL ME WE ARE BLOWING SOMETHING UP.
SORRY, WRECKER, THIS IS STRICTLY STEALTH.

UGH. I HATE THAT WORD.

ECHO, YOU'RE UP.

DON'T WORRY. AS SOON AS I PLUG IN, I'LL SEND A SIGNAL TO THE COMMAND SHIP.

WHAT TYPE OF SIGNAL ARE YOU GONNA SEND? NOTHING THAT'LL GIVE US AWAY, RIGHT?

AS FAR AS THE DROIDS ARE CONCERNED, WE'RE JUST GONNA BE ANOTHER ONE OF THEIR SHUTTLES COMING IN FOR A LANDING.

AND THE REGS THINK *WE* TAKE RISKS.

WE HAVE AN INCOMING SHIP.

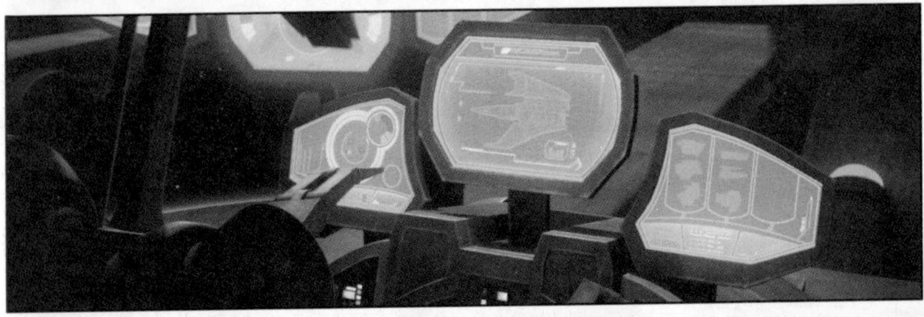

IS THIS ONE OF OURS? I'VE NEVER SEEN THIS MODEL.

SENDING THE SIGNAL... NOW.

YEP, IT'S ONE OF OURS. ROGER, ROGER, SHUTTLE TC-159. YOU MAY APPROACH AND LAND.

I'D STILL RATHER BLOW IT UP.

I HAVE A FEELING YOU'LL GET YOUR CHANCE.

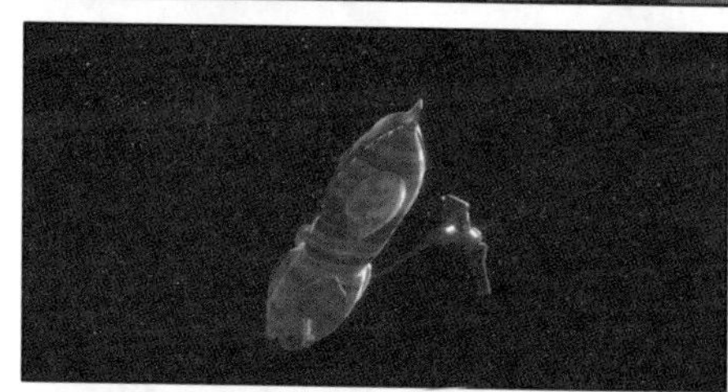

GOLD LEADER, YOU'RE CLEARED FOR LAUNCH.

COPY THAT, GENERAL. WE ARE GOING IN.

KABOOM

ADMIRAL TRENCH, THE JEDI ARE ATTACKING THE ASSEMBLY PLANT WITH A LARGE FORCE.

YES.
NOW I WILL USE
THEIR ARROGANCE AND
DESPERATION TO OUR
ADVANTAGE.

TECH, CAN YOU RIG AN INTERFACE?

I ASSUME THAT'S A RHETORICAL QUESTION.

WE SHOULD MAKE SURE THIS COMM VAULT HAS NO OTHER ENTRANCES.
I'M ON IT.

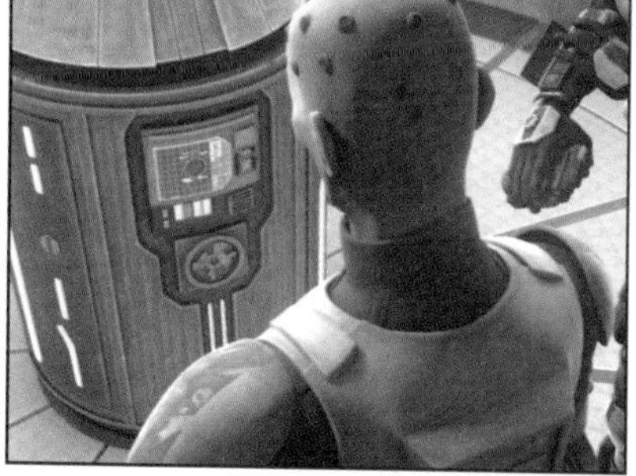

CONTACT SKAKO. I WANT TO USE THE ALGORITHM TO CALCULATE THE BEST POSSIBLE COUNTERATTACK.

AS YOU COMMAND.

ALL RIGHT, I HAVE ACCESS TO EVERYTHING, AND GOOD TIMING.

I JUST SCANNED A STRATEGY REQUEST TRENCH SENT TO THE TECHNO UNION.

WAIT. YOU CAN'T JUST SEND A SIGNAL FROM HERE.
WHY NOT?

WE HAVE TO MAKE IT APPEAR AS IF YOUR SIGNAL IS ORIGINATING FROM SKAKO MINOR. OTHERWISE THEY'LL KNOW WE ARE HERE.

MY NAME IS GENERAL MACE WINDU OF THE JEDI ORDER.

AT THIS POINT OF THE CLONE WAR, I HAVE DISMANTLED AND DESTROYED OVER 100,000 OF YOU TYPE ONE BATTLE DROIDS.

I'M GIVING YOU AN OPPORTUNITY TO PEACEFULLY LAY DOWN YOUR WEAPONS SO THAT YOU MAY BE REPROGRAMMED TO SERVE A BETTER PURPOSE THAN SPREADING THE MINDLESS VIOLENCE AND CHAOS WHICH YOU HAVE INFLICTED UPON THE GALAXY.

BLAST THEM!

WELL, I GUESS IT WAS WORTH A TRY.

HERE'S THE NEW STRATEGY FROM SKAKO, ADMIRAL. MOBILIZE ALL TROOPS ON ANAXES TO THE ASSEMBLY COMPLEX.

THE REPUBLIC WILL NOT SEND REINFORCEMENTS. THEY WILL PUT ALL THEIR FAITH IN THE JEDI.

GIVE THE ORDER.

I'M INTERCEPTING A TRANSMISSION.

TRENCH IS ORDERING ALL OF HIS DROIDS TO THE ASSEMBLY COMPLEX.

ALL RIGHT, ECHO, WHAT ARE YOU TRYING TO PULL?

DON'T WORRY, THAT'S WHAT I TOLD HIM TO DO.

BUT OUR TROOPS WILL BE VASTLY OUTNUMBERED.

NOT WHEN I SEND THEM A FEEDBACK PULSE THAT SHUTS DOWN ALL THE DROIDS.

HOW DO WE KNOW THAT'S WHAT YOU'RE REALLY GOING TO DO?

WE HAVE TO TRUST HIM.

REX IS RIGHT. ECHO, WE'RE ALL COUNTING ON YOU.

MASTER WINDU, I KNOW THIS SOUNDS CRAZY, BUT IT'S ABOUT TO GET A LITTLE MORE CROWDED WHERE YOU ARE.
WE HAVE OUR HANDS FULL AS IT IS. WHAT IS YOUR PLAN?

WELL, IF IT MAKES YOU FEEL ANY BETTER, IT ISN'T MY PLAN.
ECHO IS DRAWING ALL THE DROIDS TO YOUR POSITION, SO HE CAN NEUTRALIZE THEM ALL AT THE SAME TIME.

OBI-WAN!

SKYWALKER JUST CONTACTED ME. HE SAID WE'VE GOT A LOT MORE DROIDS HEADED OUR WAY.

I SEE ANAKIN IS BEING AS INSIGHTFUL AS EVER.

I WAS TOLD NOT TO WORRY. IT WAS ALL PART OF THEIR PLAN.

IF I KNOW ANAKIN, WE'VE GOT THE EASY PART.

THE DROIDS ARE GOING TO OVERWHELM THE JEDI. THEY DON'T STAND A CHANCE.

WELL, THERE WEREN'T AS MANY AS I THOUGHT THERE WERE GOING TO BE.

DOES THIS MEET YOUR EXPECTATIONS?
THIS EXCEEDS MY EXPECTATIONS.

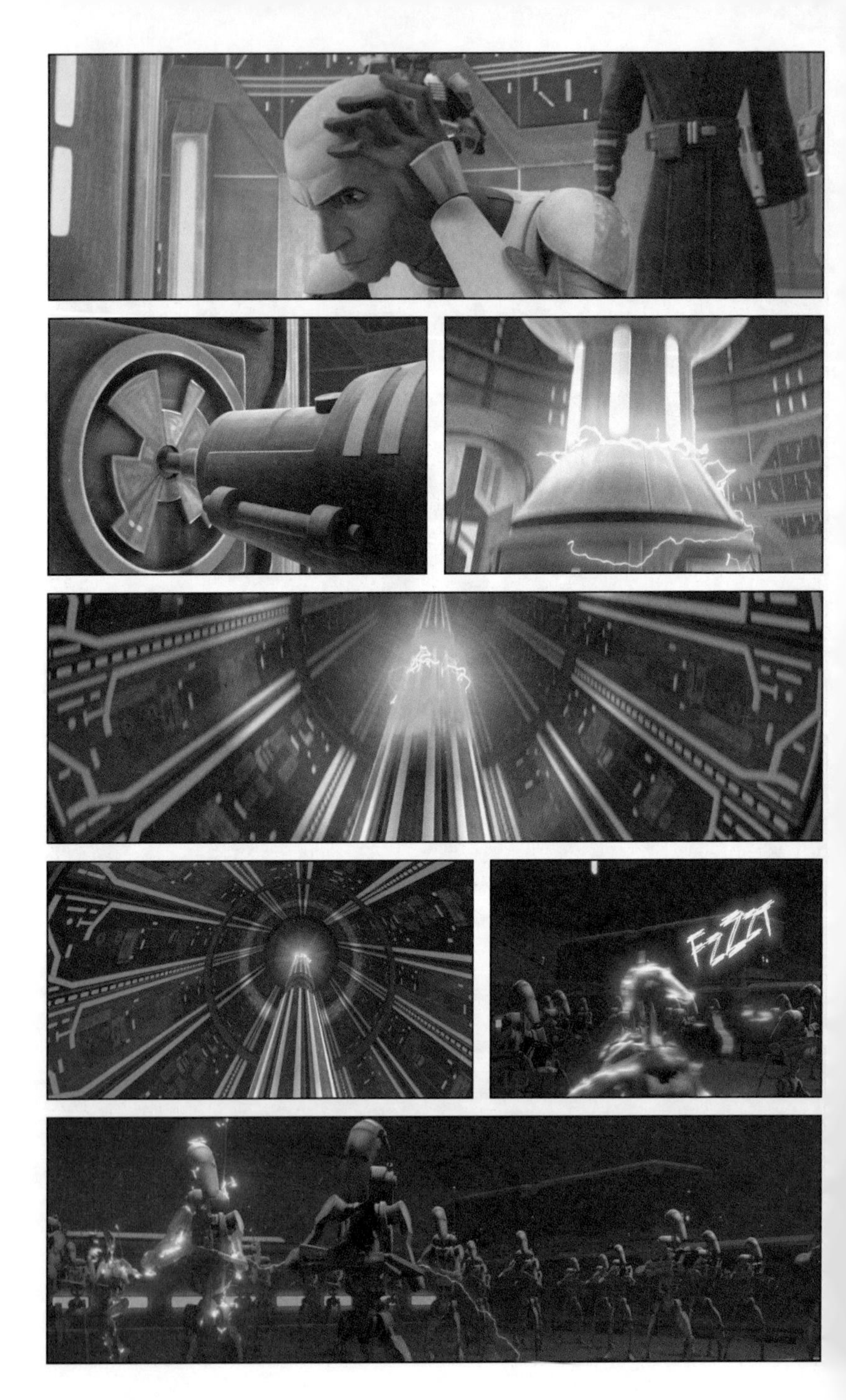
FZZZT

WHAT?

WHAT WAS THAT?

WE MONITORED A POWERFUL ENERGY SURGE, WHICH HAS OVERLOADED THE DROIDS' CIRCUITRY.

WE ARE TRACKING THE ORIGIN OF THIS PULSE NOW.

I AM PLEASED TO REPORT THAT WE ARE IN CONTROL OF THE ASSEMBLY COMPLEX, AND ALL OF THE FRONTS ARE FALLING TO THE REPUBLIC THANKS TO ECHO'S PLAN.

THAT'S GOOD NEWS, MASTER WINDU. WE'RE ON OUR WAY BACK TO THE BASE.
MAY THE FORCE BE WITH YOU.

GOOD JOB, ECHO.

WELL, I GUESS YOU ACTUALLY ARE ON OUR SIDE.

WAS THERE EVER ANY DOUBT?
SOME.

WELL, THANKS.

COME ON, BROTHER. UNPLUG, AND LET'S GET OUT OF HERE.

THE ALGORITHM HAS NEVER BEEN WRONG BEFORE. HOW COULD WE HAVE MISSED THIS?

THE SOURCE ORIGINATED ON BOARD THIS SHIP.

DISPATCH SECURITY DROIDS.

WHAT ABOUT OUR APPARENT DEFEAT?

HEH-HEH. A WISE LEADER DOES NOT RELY COMPLETELY ON THINGS SUCH AS ALGORITHMS. MY PERSONAL STRATEGY FOR VICTORY IS THROUGH TOTAL ANNIHILATION.

WAIT, I JUST SCANNED A NEW ORDER FROM TRENCH. HE'S INITIATED A COUNTDOWN.

THERE'S A BOMB HIDDEN AT THE ASSEMBLY COMPLEX, BUT IT'S BIG ENOUGH TO DESTROY MOST OF ANAXES.

CAN YOU STOP IT?

WELL, I CAN TRY.

GENERAL, WHERE ARE YOU GOING?
IF YOU CAN'T STOP THE DETONATION, PERHAPS TRENCH CAN!

CONTINUE YOUR SWEEP, JESSE.
SIR.

GENERAL WINDU, THIS IS TECH. WE'VE DISCOVERED A BOMB IN THE FUSION REACTOR. WE NEED SOMEONE TO GO DOWN THERE AND HELP DISARM IT.

I'M ON MY WAY.

GET THE MEN OUT OF HERE.

YOU HEARD GENERAL WINDU. ORGANIZE YOUR PLATOONS, AND HAVE THEM EVACUATE AS SOON AS POSSIBLE.
SIR, YES, SIR!

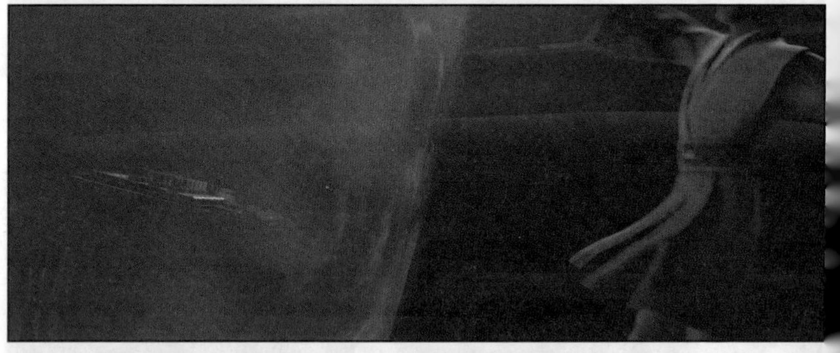

RAY SHIELD.

ECHO, I FOUND THE BOMB. TELL ME THE SEQUENCE TO SHUT IT DOWN.

I'M DECRYPTING IT NOW.

YOU HAVE TO UNPLUG. THEY'RE GOING TO DETECT US.

NO, NO, WE NEED THESE CODES.

THE FIRST NUMBER IN THE SEQUENCE IS THREE.

THE NEXT IS...ONE.
WE HAVE LOCATED THE SOURCE OF THE PULSE.
SEVEN.

JAM THE SIGNAL AT ITS SOURCE.

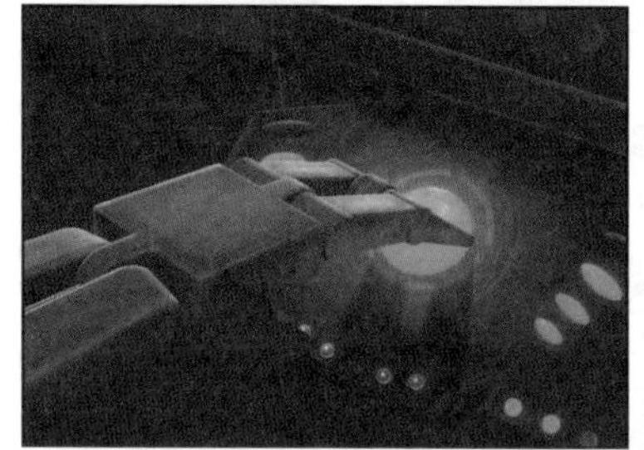

ZZZT

FZZZT

ARGH!

ECHO?

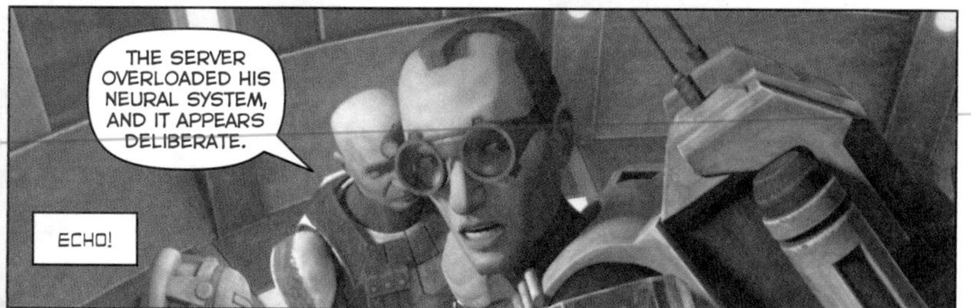
THE SERVER OVERLOADED HIS NEURAL SYSTEM, AND IT APPEARS DELIBERATE.
ECHO!

THAT MEANS TRENCH KNOWS WE'RE HERE.

ECHO, ARE YOU THERE?
GENERAL WINDU, TRENCH TOOK OUT ECHO. WE CAN'T GET YOU THE LAST NUMBER IN THE SEQUENCE.

SORRY, GENERAL, YOU'LL HAVE TO DISARM THAT BOMB WITHOUT US.
DON'T WORRY ABOUT ME, CAPTAIN. JUST GET YOUR MEN OUT OF THERE.
YES, SIR.

WE GOT COMPANY!

THE JEDI LACKS THE FINAL SEQUENCES TO STOP THE DETONATION. THE LOSS OF CLONES AT THE SHIPYARD WILL SEAL THE REPUBLIC'S FATE.

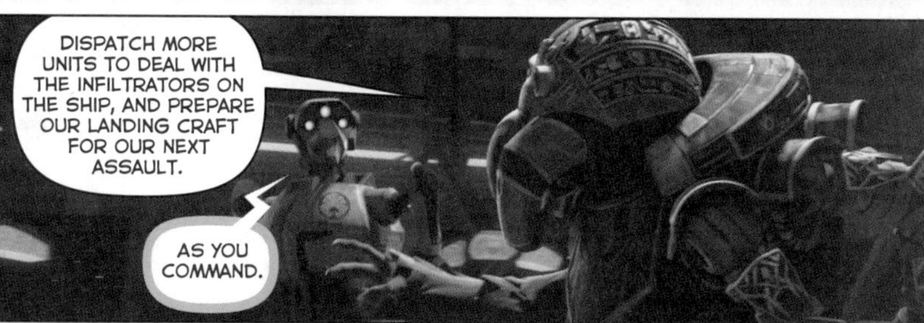
DISPATCH MORE UNITS TO DEAL WITH THE INFILTRATORS ON THE SHIP, AND PREPARE OUR LANDING CRAFT FOR OUR NEXT ASSAULT.
AS YOU COMMAND.

HUH? JEDI SCUM.

FZZT

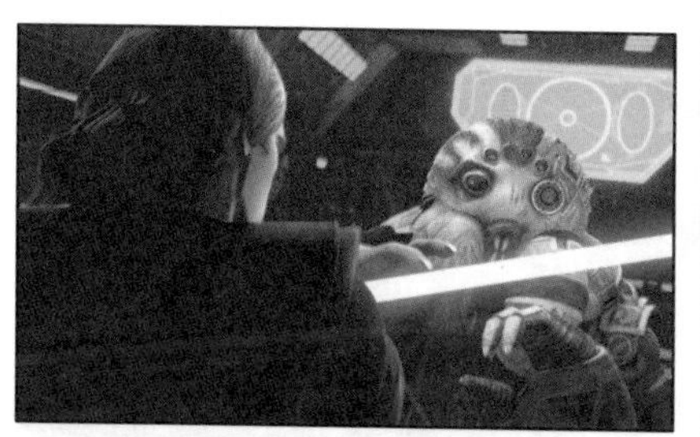

TELL ME THE SEQUENCE TO DISARM THE BOMB!

NEVER. DOOKU WOULD KILL ME FOR LOSING ANAXES.

AND YOU THINK I WON'T?

YOU'RE A JEDI. YOUR NOBILITY...

TZKT

I DON'T HAVE SUCH WEAKNESSES! NOW, LET'S TRY THAT AGAIN.

MACE, IF YOU CAN'T STOP THE DETONATION, YOU MUST LEAVE NOW.

THAT IS NOT AN OPTION. I STILL HAVE A CHANCE TO STOP THIS, EVEN IF IT'S DOWN TO MY BEST GUESS.
HOW ABOUT I TAKE THE GUESSWORK OUT OF IT, MASTER?

ADMIRAL TRENCH WAS KIND ENOUGH TO GIVE ME THE FINAL NUMBER HIMSELF. TRY SEVEN.

GOOD WORK, SKYWALKER. THE BOMB HAS BEEN DISARMED.

YOU BOTH OWE ME ONE NOW.

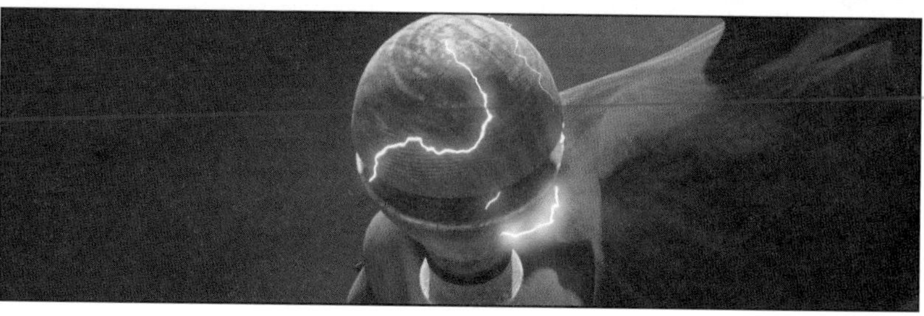

AAAH--
ZZZZT

TKZZT

WRECKER'S GONNA LOVE THIS.

ADMIRAL, IT WAS A PLEASURE.

WE CAN'T BLAST OUR WAY OUT. THERE'S TOO MANY OF THEM.

WHAT'S HE DOING?

TIME TO RELEASE THE WRECKING BALL! YEAH!

SMASH

CRASH

I HONESTLY FEEL BAD FOR THOSE DROIDS.

IT'S ALL CLEAR!

PLEASE, NOT THE FACE.

BASH

MORE DROIDS.

GO. I'LL BUY YOU SOME TIME.

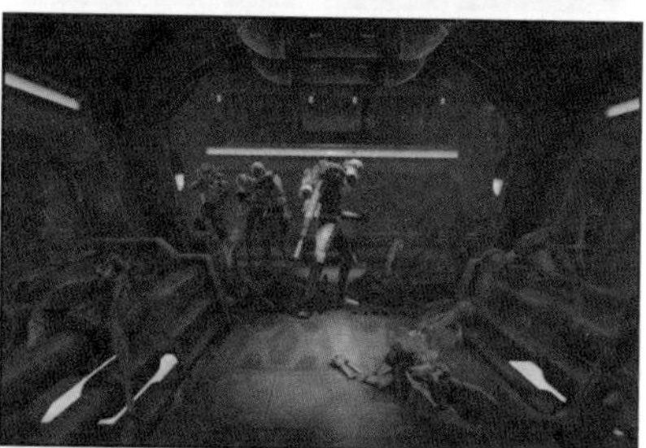

WE'LL MEET YOU AT THE INFILTRATION POINT.

OH! HE'S GONNA TRY AND TOP ME. YOU WATCH.

THIS IS THE INFILTRATION POINT.

I'M PICKING UP DOZENS OF DROIDS ON MY SENSORS, ALL HEADING THIS WAY.

HOPE YOU'RE NOT WAITING ON ME.

NOW ALL WE'RE MISSING IS CROSSHAIR.

YOU MISS ME? HOW TOUCHING.

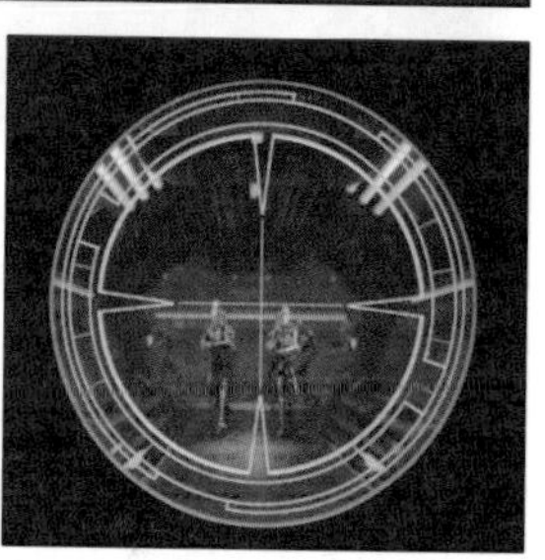

RELAX, WRECKER. YOU'LL TOP HIM NEXT TIME.

NO, HE WON'T.

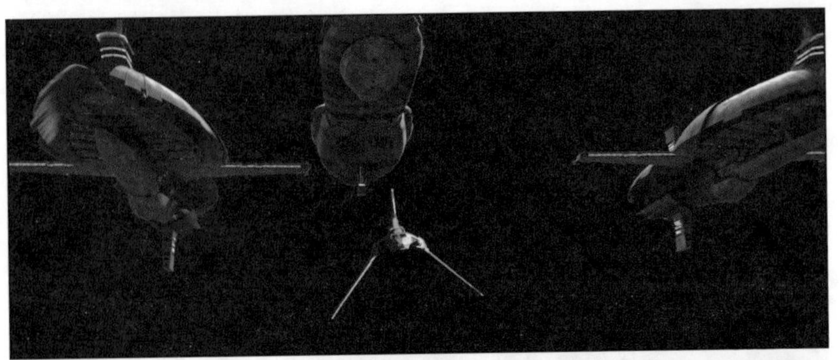

I'VE GOT A PRESENT FOR YOU, WRECKER.
OH, SERIOUSLY? I GET TO BLOW IT UP? THE WHOLE STINKING THING?

THIS IS THE HAPPIEST DAY OF MY LIFE.

KABOOM

CAPTAIN REX, CORPORAL ECHO, AND CLONE FORCE 99, YOU HAVE ALL DONE A GREAT SERVICE FOR THE REPUBLIC.

THANKS TO YOUR COURAGE AND EFFORT, REPUBLIC SHIPYARDS WILL SOON BE UP AND RUNNING AGAIN.

YOU'VE GOT SOME MEDALS COMING YOUR WAY.

THANK YOU, GENERAL.

YOU COMING?

NOT REALLY OUR THING.

ACCOLADES.

YEAH, WE'RE JUST IN IT FOR THE THRILL. YO!

YOU SURE IT'S *YOUR* THING?

WHAT DO YOU MEAN?

YOUR PATH IS DIFFERENT. LIKE OURS.

IF YOU EVER FEEL LIKE YOU DON'T FIT IN WITH THEM, WELL, FIND US.

THOSE ARE SOME OF THE FINEST TROOPERS I'VE EVER FOUGHT ALONGSIDE.

ECHO.

YOU AND I GO WAY BACK.

IF THAT'S WHERE YOU FEEL YOUR PLACE IS, THEN THAT'S WHERE YOU BELONG.

THE END

EPISODE 5
GONE WITH A TRACE

If there is no path before you,
create your own.

BETRAYAL!
JEDI PADAWAN AHSOKA TANO WAS WRONGLY ACCUSED OF TREASON BY THE JEDI COUNCIL AND HUNTED BY THE GRAND ARMY OF THE REPUBLIC.

BELIEVING HIS APPRENTICE WAS INNOCENT, ANAKIN SKYWALKER DISCOVERED THE TRUE VILLAIN WAS AHSOKA'S CLOSE FRIEND, BARRISS OFFEE.

UNABLE TO RECONCILE HER RELATIONSHIP WITH THE JEDI ORDER, AHSOKA DECIDED TO WALK AWAY FROM THE ONLY LIFE SHE HAD EVER KNOWN.

WHAT?
ZZZZT

NO, NO,
NO, NO.

STOMP

SORRY!

WHEW.
ALL RIGHT.

OH, NO.

SCREECH

WHAT A PIECE OF JUNK. NOW, HOW AM I GONNA FIX THIS?
OH! BAD CRASH. NICE ROLL, THOUGH.
THANKS... I GUESS.

THAT BIKE IS TRASH.
I DON'T KNOW WHAT I WAS THINKING WHEN I BOUGHT IT.

LOOK AT THIS MESS. THE REPULSOR BLEW. THE COMPRESSOR IS SHOT.
SOUNDS LIKE YOU KNOW A THING OR TWO ABOUT ENGINES.

I'M SORRY. WHO ARE YOU?
I'M TRACE.

AHSOKA.

AS FOR YOUR BIKE, YOU'RE IN LUCK. YOU HAPPENED TO CRASH ONTO ONE OF THE BEST REPAIR SHOPS ON 1313.
SO YOU'RE A MECHANIC?

THAT I AM, AND I'D BE GLAD TO FIX YOUR BIKE FOR A PRICE.
I CAN FIX MY OWN BIKE. I JUST NEED SOME TOOLS.

HAVE IT YOUR WAY. BUT THE TOOLS ARE STILL GONNA COST YOU.
I DON'T HAVE MUCH IN THE WAY OF CREDITS.

DON'T WORRY. DOWN HERE, NO ONE DOES. COME ON.

THAT'S A NEBULA-CLASS FREIGHTER. OR AT LEAST IT WAS.
GOOD EYE. I'M TURNING IT INTO SOMETHING WITH A BIT MORE SPEED. I THINK.

YOUR SPACE IS OVER THERE. WHY DON'T YOU GET THAT THING INSIDE AND SETTLE IN?

THANKS.

DON'T TAKE TOO LONG. TIME IS MONEY.

HEY, WHY ARE YOU HELPING ME?

SHOULDN'T I? SEEMED LIKE THE RIGHT THING TO DO. YOU CAN LEAVE IF YOU WANT.

NO. IT'S ALL RIGHT. I'LL STAY. THANK YOU.

THAT'S GOOD. I REALLY NEED THE MONEY.

HOW'S IT GOING DOWN THERE? NEED ANY HELP?

NOT IF YOU'RE GONNA CHARGE ME.

HEY, I DON'T KNOW WHERE YOU'RE FROM, BUT DOWN HERE, EVERYTHING HAS A PRICE.
IF YOU'RE GONNA STICK AROUND, YOU BETTER GET USED TO IT.

WELL, YOU MIGHT BE IN LUCK. THIS ENGINE ISN'T GOING TO RUN WITHOUT A NEW SPARKER. GOT ONE I CAN BUY?

GOT BAD NEWS. THE ONLY SPARKERS I GOT ARE RIGHT HERE. AND I AIN'T GOT NO MORE.

THAT WON'T DO. I NEED TO GET OUT OF HERE.

WHY? YOU RUNNING FROM SOMETHING?

MAYBE THIS WAS A BAD IDEA. I DON'T KNOW WHAT I'M DOING HERE.

HEY! WHAT DID I SAY? LOOK, YOU CAN STAY HERE AS LONG AS YOU LIKE.
IF YOU CAN PAY ME. WHAT'S WITH YOU?

VRROOOM

NO SENSE IN KEEPING YOU HERE IF YOU'RE GONNA BE MISERABLE.

I APPRECIATE THE HELP. WHAT'S IT GONNA COST?
IT'S ON THE HOUSE.

YOU KNOW, WHERE I COME FROM, IT'S VERY DIFFERENT FROM HERE.

OBVIOUSLY. SO WHERE DO YOU COME FROM ANYWAY?
I...UM... USED TO LIVE IN THE UPPER LEVELS OF CORUSCANT.

AH, UP THERE WHERE THE AIR IS CLEAR, HUH?
YOU'RE PROBABLY BETTER OFF DOWN HERE.

WHY'S THAT?

I'M SURE YOU HAVE YOUR PROBLEMS UP THERE WITH THE JEDI RUNNING AROUND STARTING WARS, POLICING EVERYTHING.

THE JEDI DIDN'T START THE WAR. THEY'RE TRYING TO STOP IT.

SURE. SURE, THEY ARE. LOOK, IT DOESN'T REALLY MATTER ANYWAY. THEY'VE FORGOTTEN ALL ABOUT US.

WHAT DO YOU MEAN?

IT'S JUST...WHEN YOU'RE A KID, YOU HEAR STORIES. I GUESS THEY'RE NOT WHAT I THOUGHT THEY'D BE.

IT'S NOT SAFE DOWN HERE OR ANYWHERE ON CORUSCANT. THAT'S WHY I'VE GOT MY SHIP, SO I CAN MAKE MY LIVING IN THE STARS. JUST ME AND MY SISTER, RAFA.

WE'LL GET AWAY FROM THE JEDI, THIS WAR, ALL OF IT.

MARTEZ! YOUR SISTER SAID SHE WAS PAYING ME TODAY.

WHERE IS SHE?

LET ME HANDLE THIS.
DON'T DO ANYTHING. GOT IT?

ALL RIGHT.

HEY, HEY, PINTU. RAFA SAID SHE WAS COMING TO SEE YOU.

WELL, SINCE SHE'S NOT HERE, I GUESS YOU'RE GONNA HAVE TO PAY ME INSTEAD.

I'D BACK OFF IF I WERE YOU.

STAY OUT OF THIS.

NOW, WHERE'S MY MONEY?

I GOT IT.

RIGHT...

HERE!
WHAM

BOOF

WHUMP

ON SECOND THOUGHT, SOME HELP WOULD BE GREAT.

WHOOMP

BOOF

I THINK YOU WANNA LEAVE NOW.

TELL RAFA THIS IS FAR FROM OVER.

WHOA! WHERE DID YOU LEARN TO FIGHT LIKE THAT?
MY OLDER BROTHER TAUGHT ME.
MAYBE YOU CAN TEACH ME SOMEDAY.
COME ON, WE GOTTA GO TELL MY SISTER ABOUT PINTU.

UH...

NOPE.

RAFA.
MEH.

RAFA, DOES THAT BELONG TO YOU?

NOT YET.

OH, TRACE! WHAT HAPPENED TO YOUR FACE?

PINTU CAME BY TO GET PAID. YOU WEREN'T THERE. YOU PLAN ON PAYING HIM?

I AM. I GOT A BIG JOB COMING THROUGH THAT'LL MAKE EVERYTHING GOOD FOR US.

IS IT LEGITIMATE THIS TIME OR THE USUAL JOB?

HEY, WHAT DID I TEACH YOU? WE CAN'T COUNT ON ANYONE...

SO WE COUNT ON OURSELVES. I KNOW.

THAT'S RIGHT. THAT'S HOW WE SURVIVE.

WHO IS THIS INTERESTING CREATURE?

MY NAME IS AHSOKA.

LOVELY NAME, AHSOKA.

AHSOKA, THIS IS MY SISTER, RAFA MARTEZ.
HOW'D YOU END UP WITH THIS MOOFMILKER?

SHE FELL FROM THE SKY.
I MEAN, REALLY. DROPPED RIGHT IN ON THE MECH BAY PLATFORM.

WHERE EXACTLY ARE YOU FROM?

I'M FROM TOPSIDE. YOUR SISTER'S BEEN HELPING ME OUT.

REALLY? HMM. HOW MUCH IS SHE CHARGING YOU?
NOT ENOUGH TO PAY YOUR DEBT.

NOT THAT IT'S ANY OF YOUR BUSINESS...

BUT I AM SORRY ABOUT THAT, TRACE.

YOU PROMISED YOU WOULD STAY AWAY FROM PINTU.
I NEEDED MONEY FOR THIS PLACE, FOR REPAIRS AND OTHER THINGS.

YOU COULD HAVE AT LEAST GIVEN ME A HEADS-UP THAT YOU WEREN'T GONNA PAY HIM.

YOU'RE RIGHT. WON'T HAPPEN AGAIN.

GOOD. I CAN ONLY TAKE SO MANY PUNCHES TO MY HEAD AND STILL BE CONSIDERED A PILOT.

HERE'S OUR NEXT PAYDAY.

HOW CAN I HELP YOU, MY FRIEND?

I'VE GOT THREE DROIDS THAT NEED TO BE BUILT.
MY BUSINESS PARTNER BROKERED A DEAL WITH A... RAFA MARTEZ.

YOU'RE LOOKING AT HER. AND THAT DEAL WILL BE HONORED.
THIS MAY NOT LOOK LIKE A DROID FACTORY, BUT THAT'S TO THROW OFF THE AUTHORITIES. MY ASSOCIATE DOES ASSEMBLY IN THE BACK.

WHO'S YOUR ASSOCIATE?
DON'T WORRY ABOUT THAT YET.

MY, UH, BUSINESS PARTNER, HE SAID YOU BUILD DROIDS BETTER THAN ANYBODY.

THEN THEY KNOW QUALITY. LOOK, JUST BRING THEM 'ROUND BACK.

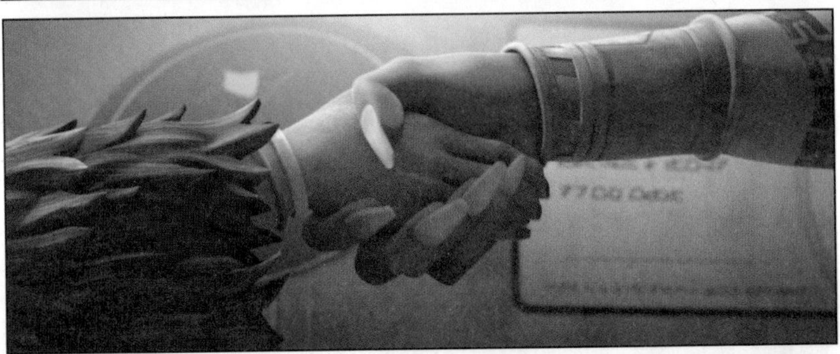

SO, TRACE, FEEL LIKE BUILDING SOME DROIDS?

IT'S BEEN A WHILE SINCE I BUILT A DROID. BUT IT'S NOT TOO DIFFICULT, JUST MORE MOVING PARTS.

JUST MAKE SURE YOU AFFIX THE RESTRAINING BOLT TO THAT PILE OF MOVING PARTS BEFORE YOU PUNCH THE POWER CYCLE.

GOT ONE RIGHT HERE. WHAT'S YOUR WORRY?

I'VE HAD MY FAIR SHARE OF RUN-INS WITH DROIDS. THE MAJORITY ARE FINE, BUT SOME ARE JUST CROSS-WIRED FROM THE START.
AND THIS IS NO ASTROMECH.

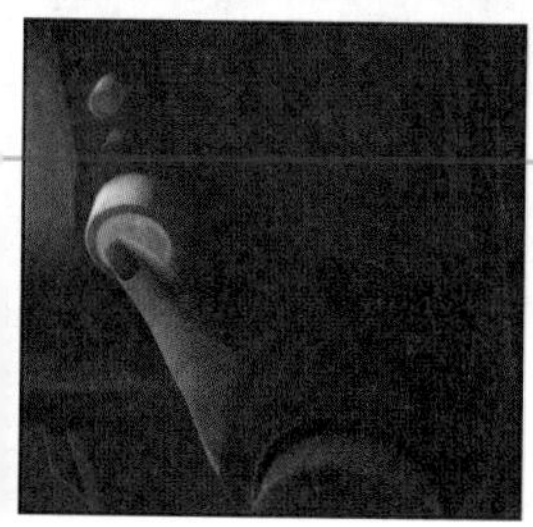

GRRRW

YOU SEEM TO KNOW A LOT ABOUT EVERYTHING.
NOT EVERYTHING. I STILL DON'T UNDERSTAND PEOPLE.

WHAT'S TO KNOW?
THERE ARE GOOD PEOPLE AND BAD PEOPLE, AND SOME ARE JUST CROSS-WIRED LIKE THIS BINARY LOAD LIFTER.

BINARY LOAD LIFTER.

WAIT A MINUTE. I DO KNOW THIS TYPE OF DROID.

GRRRWWW

CLICK
CLICK

RRRWWWWWWWWWWW

ARE YOU ALL RIGHT?
TYPE TWO LOAD LIFTERS WERE A FRAUD.

THEY WERE REPURPOSED DEMOLITION DROIDS PRONE TO VIOLENCE.

BEEP BEEP BEEP
WELL, GOOD THING WE PUT THE RESTRAINING BOLTS ON.

TRACE, THE BOLT.

WHAT THE...

NO. THAT...
THAT'S NOT...

NO, NO. NO, NO.
TRACE, THAT'S MY DROID.
WHERE'S IT GOING?

IT'S A TEST RUN. NOTHING TO WORRY ABOUT.

THIS ISN'T FUNNY, TRACE!

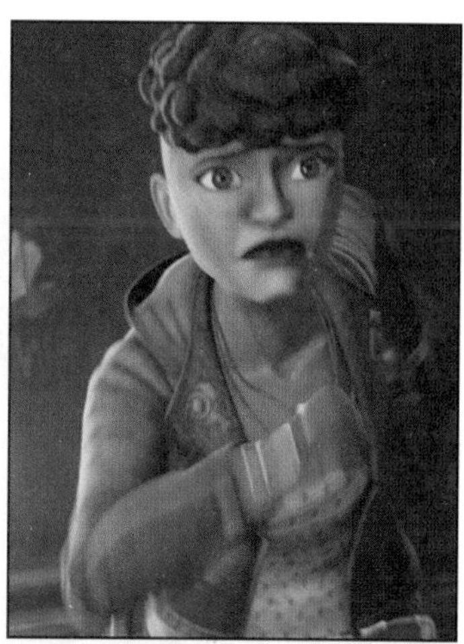

STOP!
STOP!

GRRRWWW

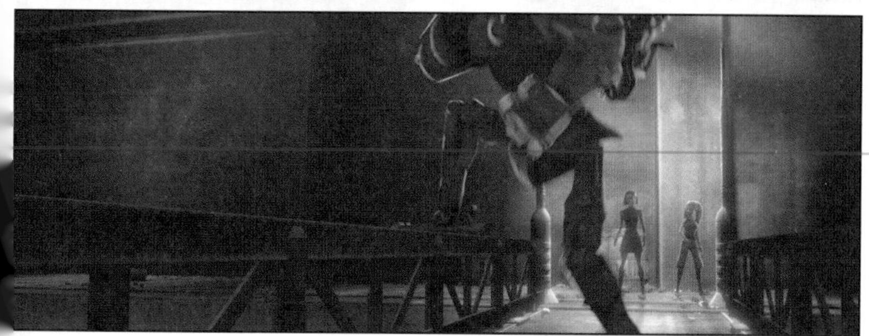

THUD

YOU SAID DEMOLITION DROID, RIGHT?
YEAH.

GO BACK TO RAFA'S AND GET THE TRACKING DEVICE FOR THAT DROID.
WHAT ARE YOU GONNA DO?
FIND A SPEEDER AND MEET YOU THERE.

WHERE'S THE DROID?

WORKING ON IT.

WHERE'S TRACE?

GOTTA GO.

TRACE, I TRUSTED YOU. WE'RE GOING TO OWE MORE CREDITS THAN WE WERE PAID FOR THIS THING!

STOP. STOP. IT'S REALLY CLOSE.

WHERE? DO YOU SEE IT?
YEAH. IT'S HEADED STRAIGHT FOR US.

THE OFF SWITCH, IT'S ON ITS FACEPLATE.

OKAY. BUT LET ME GRAB IT FIRST.

GOT IT!

SEE? NOTHING TO IT.

OH, NO. THIS WAS A BAD IDEA.
YEAH, THAT HAPPENS.

I GOTTA CUT IT LOOSE.

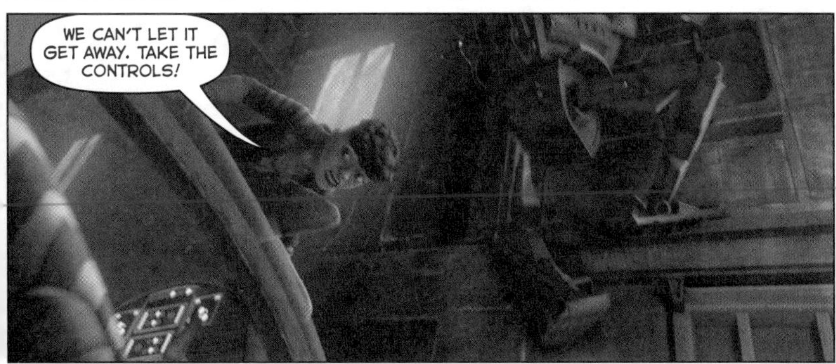
WE CAN'T LET IT GET AWAY. TAKE THE CONTROLS!

JUST
HIT THE BLUE
BUTTON.

COME ON.
COME ON!

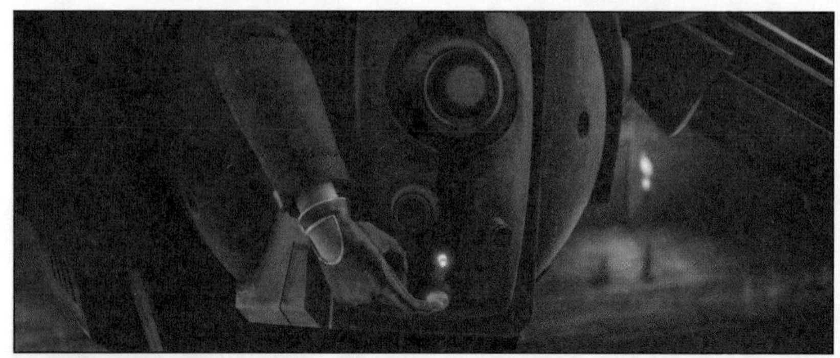

HEY, KID.
RRRWWWWWWWWWWWW....

OH, NO. OH, NO, NO, NO, NO!

CRUNCH

COME ON, YOU GOT IT.

THERE YOU GO, ALL GOOD!

BAD. BAD.

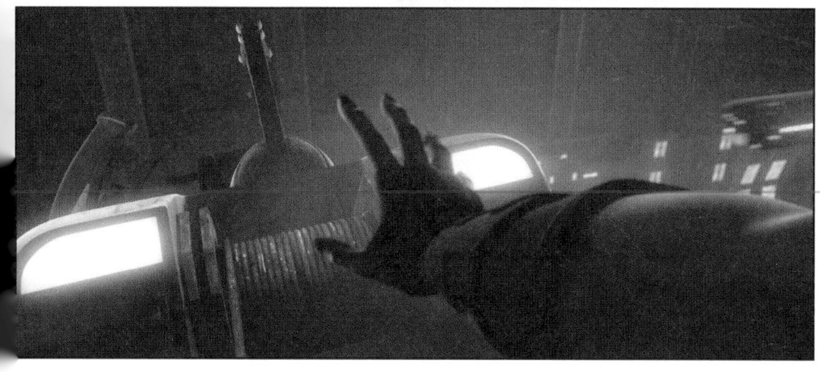

LOOK THERE. LOOK, THEY HAVE IT.

TRACE?

SEE? NOTHING TO WORRY ABOUT. WE HAD IT ALL UNDER CONTROL.

I AM NOT GOING TO DISMANTLE THOSE DROIDS.

A DEAL IS A DEAL.
THEY COULD HURT SOMEONE.

HONESTLY, NOT MY PROBLEM.
YOU DON'T KNOW WHAT THOSE DROIDS COULD BE USED FOR.
THEY'RE DANGEROUS. ONE TORE APART THE SECTOR.

WITHOUT A RESTRAINING BOLT. TRACE, DID YOU PUT THE BOLT ON ALL THREE?

YEAH, BUT WHAT IF ONE COMES OFF?

WHY IS THIS A DISCUSSION? WE ALL KNOW...

THAT YOU'RE NEW HERE.

TRACE, I'LL DO THE RIGHT THING. I'LL MEET YOU AT THE WHARF, OKAY?

RAFA, JUST BE SMART. COME ON, AHSOKA.

DO YOU EVER GET A SAY WITH RAFA?

SHE'S MY OLDER SISTER. SHE DOESN'T ALWAYS GET IT RIGHT, BUT I KNOW SHE'S TRYING TO MAKE THINGS BETTER FOR US.

AT WHAT COST?

DID YOU TELL THAT GUY ABOUT THE DROIDS?

ACTUALLY, I CHARGED THE TWI'LEK DOUBLE.

YOU GAVE THEM BACK.

YOU SAID BE SMART. LOOK, THEY WEREN'T MINE TO KEEP. WE DON'T BUILD THEM, SOMEBODY ELSE WOULD.
I DON'T GIVE THEM BACK, THAT'S MORE TROUBLE FOR THE MARTEZ SISTERS.

RAFA.
I USED THE CREDITS TO PAY OFF PINTU. IF I DIDN'T GET THE CREDITS FOR THOSE DROIDS, THEY WERE GONNA KEEP COMING AFTER US.

HERE'S ENOUGH TO BUY NEW TOOLS. THAT MAKES IT WORTH IT, RIGHT?
I GUESS SO.

STICK WITH ME, TRACE. ONE DAY, WE'LL HAVE ENOUGH CREDITS, PINTU WILL BE COMING TO US FOR WORK.

I'D BETTER GO FINISH MY SPEEDER.
YOU'RE NOT STICKING AROUND?
I THINK IT'S FOR THE BEST.

HEY.

THANKS FOR SAVING ME OUT THERE.

YOU'RE WELCOME.

NOW, LET'S GET THAT SPEEDER WORKING.
COME ON.

EPISODE 6

DEAL NO DEAL

Mistakes are valuable lessons
often learned too late.

CROSSROADS!
AFTER LEAVING THE JEDI ORDER, AHSOKA TANO FINDS HERSELF FAR AWAY FROM THE LIFE SHE ONCE KNEW.

HERE IN THE UNDERWORLD OF CORUSCANT...

...SHE MEETS TRACE MARTEZ, AN ASPIRING PILOT...

...AND HER OLDER SISTER, RAFA, A STREETWISE GAMBLER WITH LOFTY ASPIRATIONS.

IN THEIR SHORT TIME TOGETHER, AHSOKA REALIZES NOT EVERYONE SEES THE JEDI AS HEROES, A LESSON SHE ONLY RECENTLY LEARNED HERSELF.

I CAN TELL YOU'VE WORKED ON STARSHIPS BEFORE. THAT MUST HAVE BEEN SOME ACADEMY YOU WENT TO TOPSIDE.

YEAH, THE BEST.
WHAT WAS IT CALLED?
UH...SKYWALKER ACADEMY.

SKYWALKER? NEVER HEARD OF IT. BUT WHAT DO I KNOW, LIVING DOWN HERE? I NEVER REALLY HEARD OF ANY ACADEMY.
NOT LIKE I WAS EVER GONNA ATTEND ONE.

WHY NOT?

FIRST, THERE AREN'T ANY ACADEMIES DOWN HERE. SECOND, IF THERE WAS, I COULDN'T AFFORD IT.

I MEAN, LOOK AROUND. THIS IS IT.

RAFA AND I INHERITED THIS HANGAR AFTER OUR PARENTS...SPLIT.

AND THE SHOP RAFA OWNS? SHE WON IT GAMBLING SO SHE COULD USE IT AS A FRONT FOR HER SCHEMES.

WHERE'D YOU GET THE SHIP?

THIS? THIS IS ME. I DID ODD JOBS, MECH WORK, WHATEVER I COULD TO MAKE SOME CREDITS, AND ASSEMBLED IT PIECE BY PIECE.

ALL THAT, PLUS RAFA CHIPPING IN. AND NOW I'VE GOT MYSELF A STARSHIP.

IMPRESSIVE.
NO, IMPRESSIVE IS COMING UP. ONCE THE *SILVER ANGEL* REVS UP ITS HYPERDRIVE.

THE *SILVER ANGEL*?
YEAH, WHY?
I DON'T KNOW. I JUST NEVER HEARD A NAME LIKE THAT BEFORE.

WAIT, YOU'RE SAYING IT'S A BAD NAME?
HEY, IT'S YOUR SHIP, YOU CALL IT WHAT YOU WANT.

WHY DON'T YOU NAME MY BIKE WHILE YOU'RE AT IT?
I DID. *TRASH*.
ITS NAME IS *TRASH*.

VERY FUNNY.

SO, ONCE YOU'RE DONE, WHERE ARE YOU HEADED?
I DON'T KNOW. THIS IS ALL NEW TO ME.

THAT'S WHY YOU SHOULD STICK AROUND.
I FIGURED I'D BE ON MY OWN FOR A BIT.
YEAH, THAT DOESN'T SEEM LIKE THE BEST IDEA.

I MEAN, YOU CRASHED HERE ON THAT PIECE OF JUNK. WHAT IF YOU DIDN'T CRASH ON MY LANDING PLATFORM?
THINGS COULD'VE GOTTEN MESSY FOR YOU.

BELIEVE ME, THINGS COULDN'T BE A BIGGER MESS FOR ME THAN THEY ALREADY ARE.

SO YOU'LL STAY A LITTLE WHILE LONGER, AT LEAST. THAT WAY WE CAN TEST THE *SILVER ANGEL*.

ALL RIGHT, AS LONG AS RAFA DOESN'T MIND.

AS LONG AS RAFA DOESN'T MIND WHAT?

AHSOKA'S GONNA BE STAYING ON FOR A BIT.

YOU GOT ANY SKILLS?

ONLY USEFUL ONES.

WE'LL FIND OUT SOON ENOUGH.

WHAT'S UP?

LOOK, I WOULDN'T ASK YOU TO DO THIS, BUT I'M IN A TOUGH SPOT.

I HIRED A STARSHIP AND CREW FOR A JOB.
YOU WHAT? YOU WERE GONNA LEAVE ME HERE?

NO, I WAS GONNA DO A JOB, MAKE US SOME MONEY, AND BE BACK.
BUT THEN THE PILOT BACKED OUT AND TOOK HIS SHIP WITH HIM, AND--

I DON'T KNOW WHAT'S WORSE.
THAT YOU WERE GONNA DO THIS OR THAT YOU HIRED A PILOT OTHER THAN ME TO DO IT WITH.

WELL, NOW I NEED YOU.

ONLY AS A BACKUP.

WHAT'S THE JOB?
I'LL TELL YOU ONCE WE'RE UNDERWAY.

I STILL HAVEN'T AGREED TO IT.

TRACE, PLEASE, I NEED YOUR HELP WITH THIS.

YOU MEAN, YOU NEED THE BEST PILOT AROUND AND THE FASTEST SHIP YOU KNOW?
YES, TO BOTH OF THOSE.

WHO LOOKS OUT FOR YOU, HUH?
YOU DO, RAFA.

THAT'S RIGHT. REMEMBER, WE CAN'T COUNT ON ANYONE.

SO WE COUNT ON OURSELVES.
AND MAYBE AHSOKA.

MAYBE.

COME ON. I WANNA GET GOING. GO WARM THE ENGINES UP.

YOU SHOW UP OUTTA NOWHERE, SUDDENLY YOU AND MY SISTER ARE INSEPARABLE?
WHAT ARE YOU AFTER?

EXCUSE ME?

COME ON. EVERYONE PLAYS AN ANGLE. I DON'T MIND, EXCEPT WHEN IT INVOLVES TRACE. SO TELL ME, WHAT ARE YOU AFTER? HER MECH-BAY? HER SHIP?

I DON'T HAVE AN ANGLE, UNLESS MAYBE TO KEEP YOU BOTH OUT OF TROUBLE.

HMM. YOU EVER THOUGHT YOU MIGHT BE THE TROUBLE SHE NEEDS TO STAY AWAY FROM?

AHSOKA, RAFA, WELCOME ABOARD THE... THE *SILVER ANGEL*.

THE *SILVER ANGEL?* YOU SHOULD RETHINK THAT.
THAT'S WHAT I TOLD HER.

UGH, JUST STRAP IN.

TRACE, WHERE ARE YOU GOING?
I'M JUST TRYING TO GET INTO THIS LANE.

THAT'S A MILITARY LANE. YOU CAN'T GO THERE. THAT'S A RESTRICTED AREA.

WE'RE BEING HAILED.
DON'T ANSWER THAT.
BEEP BEEP

WE HAVE TO ANSWER THAT.
NO, WE DON'T.

TRACE, JUST GET US OUT OF HERE.

DON'T DO ANYTHING THAT MAKES US LOOK SUSPICIOUS.
WE ALREADY LOOK SUSPICIOUS.

FLY HIGHER.
STOP TELLING ME WHAT TO DO.

PULL UP. PULL UP!

STOP TELLING ME WHAT TO DO.

BEEP
BEEP
BEEP
DON'T ANSWER THAT.

THIS IS THE *SILVER ANGEL*. WHAT CAN I DO FOR YOU?

HAVE YOU LOST YOUR MIND? THIS IS MILITARY AIRSPACE. CIVILIAN TRANSPORTS ARE NOT AUTHORIZED TO BE IN THIS SECTOR. I'LL HAVE YOUR STAR PILOT LICENSE FOR THIS!

LICENSE? DO I NEED ONE OF THOSE?

UH, SORRY. SO--SO SORRY. IT WON'T HAPPEN AGAIN. JUST TEACHING MY YOUNGER SISTER TO FLY.

OH, YOU'RE TEACHING *ME* TO FLY? THAT'S A LAUGH.

WHO IS THIS? WHAT'S YOUR LICENSE NUMBER?

JUST GET IN THE TRANSPORT LANE AND FLY.

WHO WAS ON BOARD THAT TRANSPORT?

OH, JUST SOME ROOKIE PILOTS, APPARENTLY ON THEIR FIRST MANEUVERS.
I WAS JUST ABOUT TO SEND A DETACHMENT TO ARREST THEM.

SHOULD I SEND A DETACHMENT, GENERAL?

NO. IT'S NOTHING.

YOU STILL HAVEN'T TOLD US WHERE WE'RE GOING.

SHE DOESN'T LIKE SURPRISES, I SEE.

REALLY? HOW'D YOU MANAGE THAT?

THIS IS WHAT I WAS WORKING TOWARDS. TAKE US OUT, CAPTAIN.

THIS IS EXCITING. I'VE NEVER BEEN TO HYPERSPACE BEFORE.

WHAT? WHAT HAVE YOU BEEN FLYING?

OH, MAINLY SPEEDERS, YOU KNOW, MAINTENANCE VEHICLES. WHATEVER I COULD GET MY HANDS ON.

SEE WHY I TRIED TO HIRE A DIFFERENT PILOT? TRACE'S FLYING IS MORE OF A DREAM THAN A REALITY.

WHAT DID YOU SAY?

OH, I--I SAID THE SHIP FLIES LIKE A DREAM.

YEAH, A BAD ONE.

WHAT?

CLANG
BANG
OH...I LEFT THE AIR BRAKES ON. THAT COULD'VE BEEN BAD.

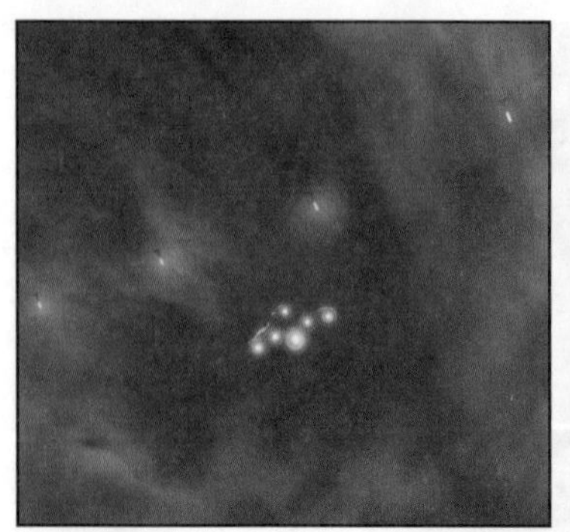

KESSEL. YOU'RE TAKING US TO KESSEL?

I'M TAKING US TO FORTUNE AND GLORY.

I'VE HEARD PILOTS TALK ABOUT THIS PLACE. IT'S LEGENDARY.

YEAH, IT'S LEGENDARY FOR ITS CORRUPTION.
RAFA, WHAT ARE WE DOING HERE?

PICKING UP MEDICINE.

THIS PLACE IS BEAUTIFUL.

SEE, AHSOKA, THERE'S NOTHING TO WORRY ABOUT.

WHICH ONE OF YOU IS RAFA MARTEZ?

I AM.

I AM KINASH LOCK, KING YARUBA'S MAJORDOMO. WE'VE BEEN EXPECTING YOU.
WE'VE PREPARED A BANQUET TO SHOW HIS THANKS FOR YOUR SERVICES.

LEAD THE WAY, SIR.

WELCOME TO THE BIG TIME.

SO, WHEN IS THE KING SHOWING?

HE LEAVES MATTERS LIKE THIS TO ME. HOWEVER, IF YOU SHOW YOURSELF TO BE DEPENDABLE, YOU WILL HAVE THE OPPORTUNITY TO MEET HIS ROYAL HIGHNESS.

WE WON'T DISAPPOINT.

I'VE GOT ONE OF THE FASTEST SHIPS AROUND.

WHAT KIND OF MEDICINE ARE WE TRANSPORTING?

THE ESSENCE OF THE MEDICINE. YOU WILL DELIVER THREE CONTAINERS OF UNREFINED SPICE.

UPON SATISFACTORY DELIVERY, YOU WILL BE AWARDED A FULL SHIPMENT AND A CONTRACT TO TRANSPORT FOR US ON A CONTINUAL BASIS.

MAY AS WELL GET THAT CONTRACT READY.

'CAUSE WE'VE GOT THE FASTEST SHIP AROUND.

THEY KNOW, TRACE.

WE'RE WORKING FOR A KING.

MANY THINGS CAN BE MADE OUT OF SPICE, AND THEY'RE NOT ALL GOOD.

I'M NOT SURE WHAT YOU MEAN. IN THIS TIME OF WAR, OUR SPICE IS REFINED INTO A MEDICINE THAT SAVES PEOPLE ACROSS THE GALAXY.

THE YARUBA FAMILY OF KESSEL HAS ALWAYS BEEN A PROMOTER OF HEALTH AND HAPPINESS ACROSS THE STARS.

NOW, COME, MS. MARTEZ.

LET US GET THE SPICE INTO THIS VERY FAST SHIP.

RUNNING SPICE IS DANGEROUS. THE TRANSPORT SHIPS GET ATTACKED OFTEN.

YEAH, BY PIRATES LOOKING FOR A QUICK SCORE. BUT THEY ALWAYS GO AFTER THE BIGGER KESSEL TRANSPORT SHIPS, OBVIOUS TARGETS.

THAT'S WHY THE KING HIRED US. WE DON'T FIT THE DESCRIPTION OF YOUR NORMAL TRANSPORT.

BUT WE'RE LEAVING KESSEL. IT'S NOT HARD TO FIGURE OUT WHAT WE MIGHT BE HERE FOR.
YOU KNOW A LOT ABOUT KESSEL FOR A MECHANIC.
I'VE HEARD THE STORIES.

THEN YOU BETTER HOPE THE PILOT OF THE *SILVER ANGEL* IS AS GOOD AS SHE SAYS SHE IS.

I'M STARTING TO SEE WHY RAFA DIDN'T ORIGINALLY HIRE YOU FOR THIS JOB. IT'S DANGEROUS.

THAT'S JUST YOUR NERVES TALKING.

NO, I'M SERIOUS. RUNNING SPICE IS NO SIMPLE TRANSPORT MISSION.

RAFA LOOKS OUT FOR ME. SURE, I WASN'T HER FIRST CHOICE FOR THIS JOB. BUT SHE WOULDN'T HAVE ASKED ME TO DO IT IF SHE DIDN'T BELIEVE I COULD.

HOW MANY TIMES HAS RAFA DONE A JOB LIKE THIS?

I DON'T THINK SHE EVER HAS.

SO HOW CAN SHE POSSIBLY KNOW WHAT WE'RE UP AGAINST?

HEY, THERE'S A FIRST TIME FOR EVERYTHING.

WE'RE COMING UP ON THE MINING ZONE.

NOW, THIS LOOKS LIKE THE KESSEL FROM THE STORIES.

SPICE MINING HAS MADE THE PEOPLE OF KESSEL WEALTHY. THERE'S ALWAYS A PRICE TO BE PAID.
THERE'S THE PLATFORM NOW.

LOOK AT ALL THOSE DROIDS.

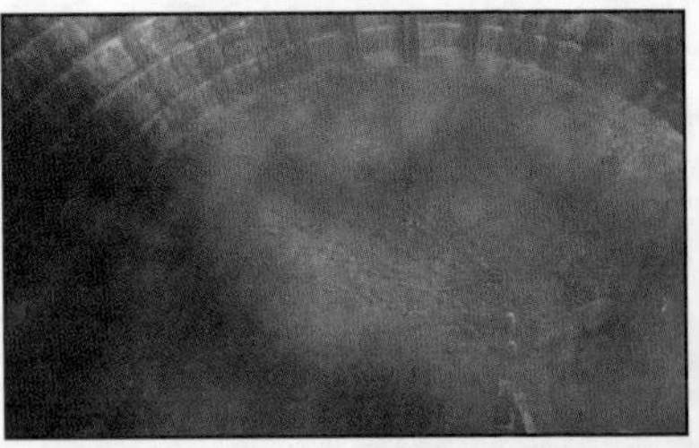

THE KING'S SPICE SALES MUST BUY THOUSANDS OF THEM.

TRACE, THOSE ARE NOT DROIDS. THEY'RE PEOPLE.

MUST BE LOCAL WORKERS.
I THINK THE TERM IS SLAVES.
CAN'T BE. AN OPERATION THIS LARGE, THE REPUBLIC WOULDN'T STAND FOR IT. THEY'D SHUT THE PLACE DOWN.

YEAH, YOU'D THINK THEY WOULD.

YOU'RE ALL READY TO DEPART.

AHSOKA, LET'S GO MAKE SURE THEY SECURE THE BINS.

I'M NOT SURE IF I LIKE HER OR NOT.

YOU NEVER LIKE ANY OF MY FRIENDS.

SHE'S NOT FAMILY, TRACE. REMEMBER THAT.

I'LL KEEP AN EYE ON HER. YOU JUST DO YOUR JOB.

KID, I GOT US A JOB. THE REST IS UP TO YOU. NOW, LET'S GET THIS SPICE WHERE IT BELONGS.

NEXT STOP OBA DIAH, RIGHT?

OBA DIAH, INDEED. MARG KRIM BETTER HAVE MY MONEY WAITING.
MARG KRIM? THE PYKE CRIME BOSS?

WHY AM I NOT SURPRISED YOU KNOW ABOUT THE PYKES?

AS A MATTER OF FACT, HOW *DO* YOU KNOW ABOUT THE PYKES?

I KNOW YOU CAN'T MAKE A DEAL WITH THEM.

ALREADY DID. TRACE, HOW DOES SHE KNOW SO MUCH?

HOW DO YOU KNOW SO MUCH?

I PAY ATTENTION TO THE WORLD AROUND ME, LIKE THE FACT THAT THE PYKES ARE GANGSTERS.

GANGSTERS? WHAT, LIKE PINTU BACK ON CORUSCANT?

NO. MUCH WORSE. GALACTICALLY WORSE. THEY'LL TAKE YOUR SHIP, YOUR LIFE, EVERYTHING!
MY SHIP?

WELL, I TOOK A JOB, AHSOKA. WE NEED ALL THE CREDITS WE CAN GET.

THIS IS BAD, TRACE.

RAFA, WHAT ARE THEY GONNA DO TO MY SHIP?

NOTHING! SEE, THIS IS WHY I DIDN'T WANT YOU FOR THIS JOB.

I WOULDN'T BRING THAT UP RIGHT NOW IF I WERE YOU.

WHY NOT MAKE THE BEST OF A BAD SITUATION AND DELIVER THIS SPICE TO SOMEPLACE THAT CAN USE IT FOR MEDICINE?

NO ONE IS TAKING MY SHIP.

BECAUSE THAT DOESN'T PAY, AND TRACE AND I HAVE A LOT OF PEOPLE ON CORUSCANT WAITING FOR MONEY WE OWE THEM.

NO. *YOU* OWE THEM, NOT HER.

SISTERS TAKE CARE OF EACH OTHER. WE CAN'T PAY OFF DEBT WITH YOUR MORALITY.

NO ONE IS TAKING MY SHIP.

THINK OF ALL THE GOOD YOU COULD DO IF WE DELIVERED THE SPICE TO SOMEPLACE ELSE INSTEAD OF THE PYKES.

THINK OF ALL THE GOOD YOU CAN DO BY HELPING US FINISH THIS JOB.

I SAID, NO ONE IS TAKING MY SHIP!

WOOSH

WHAT WAS THAT?

WHAT DID YOU DO?

I DUMPED THE SPICE.

YOU DID *WHAT*?

PROBLEM SOLVED. NEITHER ONE OF YOU GETS YOUR WAY. AND I KEEP MY SHIP.
YOU'RE WELCOME.

OF ALL THE CHOICES YOU COULD MAKE, THAT IS LITERALLY THE WORST ONE.

I CAN'T BELIEVE THIS, BUT I AGREE WITH HER.

WHAT?
THE SPICE GAVE US OPTIONS. NOW--

NOW WE HAVE A DEAL TO DELIVER SPICE TO AN INTERGALACTIC CRIME SYNDICATE AND NO SPICE TO DELIVER.

BUT I THOUGHT DELIVERING SPICE TO GANGSTERS WAS A BAD THING.

IT IS. BUT YOU HAVE TO PAY THEM SOMEHOW. RIGHT NOW, WE OWE THE PYKES.

THEN HOW WAS TURNING THE SPICE INTO MEDICINE GONNA SOLVE ANYTHING?

WELL, THAT WAS MORE OF AN ETHICAL DEBATE. I HADN'T FIGURED OUT HOW TO SOLVE THE PYKE PROBLEM YET.

YOU TWO ARE JUST A PAIR, THAT'S FOR SURE. I'LL TELL YOU WHAT, I CAN THINK OF ONE WAY TO PAY OFF THE PYKES. AND I'M STANDING IN IT.

NO ONE IS TOUCHING MY SHIP.

YOU SHOULD HAVE THOUGHT OF THAT BEFORE YOU DUMPED 30,000 CREDITS WORTH OF SPICE INTO SPACE.

STOP IT, BOTH OF YOU. I SAID I DIDN'T HAVE IT FIGURED OUT YET!

OH, BUT YOU DO NOW?

WE'LL FIND OUT.

OKAY. DO WE NEED TO GO OVER IT AGAIN?

NOPE. BECAUSE NO MATTER HOW MANY TIMES WE GO OVER IT, I CAN TELL YOU, IT'S NOT GOING TO WORK.
WHY?

BECAUSE IT'S A BAD PLAN.

IT IS A PRETTY BAD PLAN.

I'M SORRY. DID EITHER OF YOU HAVE A BETTER ONE?

WELL, THEN, SOUNDS LIKE MY PLAN IS THE BEST ONE WE GOT.

THAT'S NOT REALLY ADDRESSING WHETHER OR NOT IT'S GONNA WORK.

DON'T WORRY. I'VE GOT A TRICK OR TWO THAT YOU DON'T KNOW ABOUT.

CARE TO SHARE?

NO. NOT YET, AT LEAST.

I ASSUME THAT
YOU HAD NO TROUBLE
TRANSPORTING THE SPICE
FROM KESSEL?

NOT AT ALL. THIS IS ONE OF THE SMOOTHEST JOBS I'VE EVER HAD.

HMM. GOOD. IF ANYTHING HAD HAPPENED, IT WOULD HAVE BEEN VERY UNFORTUNATE FOR YOU.

HERE IS YOUR PAYMENT.

NOW, LET US TAKE A LOOK AT THAT CARGO.

YOU DON'T TRUST ME? I MEAN, YOU HIRED ME.

I DON'T TRUST ANYONE WHO ISN'T A PYKE.

YOU WANT TO PAY US OUR CREDITS AND SEND US ON OUR WAY.

HERE ARE YOUR CREDITS. NOW, GO ON YOUR WAY.

I TAKE IT BACK. I'M LIKING THIS PLAN.

THIS IS HIGHLY IRREGULAR. I'M GOING TO MAKE SURE EVERYTHING SORTS OUT TO OUR LIKING.

THANKS FOR EVERYTHING. WE'LL HOPEFULLY SEE YOU SOON.

FIRE UP THE SHIP.

JUST A MOMENT.
I NEED THE CODE TO UNLOCK THE BIN.

UH...I THINK WE TRANSMITTED THAT TO YOU ALREADY.

LET'S GET OUT OF HERE, TRACE.

TAP
TAP
TAP

PTHEW

WHERE IS THE SPICE?

WHAT? I DON'T BELIEVE IT. KESSEL MUST HAVE DOUBLE-CROSSED YOU. WELL, THAT'S REALLY UNFORTUNATE.

I WANT PATROL SHIPS TO CUT THEM OFF. ENGAGE THE TRACTOR BEAM.

YOU BETTER GET US OUT OF HERE NOW.

PATROL SHIPS.
THEY WON'T BE ABLE TO KEEP UP.

RUMBLE

WHAT WAS THAT?

THAT IS A TRACTOR BEAM, RAFA.

JUST SO YOU KNOW, WHEN THEY INTERROGATE ME, I'M BLAMING THE WHOLE THING ON YOU.

BETWEEN THE THREE OF US, THERE'S PLENTY OF BLAME TO GO AROUND.

TO BE CONTINUED...

CREDITS

CREATED BY GEORGE LUCAS

THE BAD BATCH

Executive Producer
and Supervising Director
Dave Filoni

Directed by
Kyle Dunlevy

Written by
Matt Michnovetz
Brent Friedman

Producer
Caroline Robinson Kermel

Co-Producer
Carrie Beck

Associate Producer
Josh Rimes

A DISTANT ECHO

Executive Producer
and Supervising Director
Dave Filoni

Directed by
Steward Lee

Written by
Matt Michnovetz
Dave Filoni
Brent Friedman

Producer
Caroline Robinson Kermel

Co-Producer
Carrie Beck

Associate Producer
Josh Rimes

ON THE WINGS OF KEERADAKS

Executive Producer
and Supervising Director
Dave Filoni

Directed by
Bosco Ng

Written by
Matt Michnovetz
Brent Friedman

Producer
Caroline Robinson Kermel

Co-Producer
Carrie Beck

Associate Producer
Josh Rimes

UNFINISHED BUSINESS

Executive Producer
and Supervising Director
Dave Filoni

Directed by
Brian Kalin O'Connell

Written by
Matt Michnovetz
Brent Friedman

Producer
Caroline Robinson Kermel

Co-Producer
Carrie Beck

Associate Producer
Josh Rimes

GONE WITH A TRACE

Executive Producer
and Supervising Director
Dave Filoni

Directed by
Saul Ruiz
Kyle Dunlevy

Written by
Dave Filoni
Charles Murray

Producer
Caroline Robinson Kermel

Co-Producer
Carrie Beck

Associate Producer
Josh Rimes

DEAL NO DEAL

Executive Producer
and Supervising Director
Dave Filoni

Directed by
Nathaniel Villanueva
Steward Lee

Written by
Dave Filoni
Charles Murray

Producer
Caroline Robinson Kermel

Co-Producer
Carrie Beck

Associate Producer
Josh Rimes